THE
LAST RESORT

THE
LAST RESORT

PETER ELEBASH

TATE PUBLISHING
AND **ENTERPRISES**, LLC

This book is designed to provide accurate and authoritative information with regard to the subject matter covered. This information is given with the understanding that neither the author nor Tate Publishing, LLC is engaged in rendering legal, professional advice. Since the details of your situation are fact dependent, you should additionally seek the services of a competent professional.

The opinions expressed by the author are not necessarily those of Tate Publishing, LLC.

Published by Tate Publishing & Enterprises, LLC
127 E. Trade Center Terrace | Mustang, Oklahoma 73064 USA
1.888.361.9473 | www.tatepublishing.com

Tate Publishing is committed to excellence in the publishing industry. The company reflects the philosophy established by the founders, based on Psalm 68:11,
"The Lord gave the word and great was the company of those who published it."

Book design copyright © 2014 by Tate Publishing, LLC. All rights reserved.
Cover design by Rtor Maghuyop
Interior design by Caypeeline Casas

Published in the United States of America

ISBN: 978-1-63306-407-2
Biography & Autobiography / General
14.09.12

To Jane, who helped me turn my life around

An engaging and extraordinarily honest story of how a Yale education does not shield you from the pitfalls of life but helps you overcome them. The glamour of selling real estate in the sun, riding polo ponies at breakneck speed and shedding wives along the way has ensured Peter Elebash has led a vivid life, tempered now in later years by his faith in God. It makes for a fascinating tale.

– Richard Evans, Author & Editor

"This book tells the fascinating story of a great American. Inspirational and highly recommended."

– Larkin Spivey
Lt. Col. U. S. Marine Corps (ret)

Military historian, speaker, and author of: God in the Trenches Miracles of the American Revolution (Gold Medal-Military Writers Society of America) Battlefields and Blessings: Stories of Faith and Courage from World War II (Silver Medal-Military Writers Society of America /Gold Medal-Stars & Flags Book Award) Stories of Faith and Courage from the Vietnam War (Gold Medal-Stars & Flags Book Award) Stories of Faith and Courage from the Korean War www.larkinspivey.com

I salute you Peter for being "all in" in using the fourth quarter of your life to serve God's purposes and challenge others to do likewise.
– Bill Hobbs, President/Founder
Urban Youth Impact

The Peter Elebash story is one of resilience, with every twist and turn leading him deeper into trust in Jesus Christ as Lord. It is also an American story of North and South, rich and poor, hard work and good times. This book will affect you for the good.
– Richardson Schell,
Headmaster of the Kent School, Kent, CT

"This is an amazing story of life transformation. After decades of ups and downs, Peter's life is now grounded and at peace because of the work of Jesus in his life. The story will challenge you and encourage you."

– Tom Lane,
Board Member, New Canaan Society

ACKNOWLEDGMENTS

Charles Hill

Charlie was a career foreign service officer who now heads "Studies in Grand Strategies" at Yale. After drinks and much discussion at Mory's, he urged me to write it down. Charlie was the catalyst for me to embark on this task.

Owen Williams

Owen recently published his story, *Ahead of the Game*. As the number one tennis player in South Africa in the 1950s, he went on to a fascinating career in tennis promotion and marketing. We have been friends for forty years, and his book gave me confidence that I could write something worth reading about my life.

Richard Evans

Richard has been covering tennis since the 1960s, and has authored fifteen books, including the official history of the Davis Cup. As my editor, he helped me organize the material, polish the text, and keep my facts straight on tennis matters.

MY HONOR ROLL

These are the people that had the greatest effect on my life:

My parents, Edgar and Wilmer Elebash. They allowed me to leave home at age seventeen.

LeGrand Elebash Jr. He fundamentally changed my life by sending me to Choate.

Seymour St. John. He was a wonderful role model as Choate's Headmaster.

Kathleen Hudson. She partnered with me, bringing two special children into the world.

Pat McKinney. He showed me how to be a successful manager of people.

Bill Ylvisaker. By creating Palm Beach Polo, he created a stage on which many of us danced.

Peter Brant. He gave me exceptional career opportunities.

Everett Cook, Eliot Clarke, and Farnham Collins. They were the catalysts for my Millbrook career.

My wife of thirteen years, Jane. Our motto is "Fourth time's the charm."

CONTENTS

PREFACE

This is the story of one man's journey to faith. The idea for the title, *The Last Resort*, came to me in the latter stages of writing, as I realized that most of my career involved working with residential resort developments in a sales and marketing capacity. All told, there were at least six such developments at various stages. At every stop, I learned something to take to the next assignment. As you will see, this was a frantic chase toward some definition of success, as defined by one's social status and financial prowess. In the end, the "last resort" for me was finding the good news of the Gospel message. Given where I started, it could have turned out much worse. I am eternally grateful to those people along the way from whom I learned what—and what not—to do. I have been blessed by the journey, and by the condition in which I find myself in today. I hope you enjoy the story, and perhaps become aware of some stones in the pathway over which I tripped, and which you may avoid by hearing my story.

INTRODUCTION

There is a tide in the affairs of men
Which, taken at the flood, leads on to fortune

—Cassius in *Julius Caesar*

As a the result of the generosity of an aptly named cousin, LeGrand Elebash, I rode my tide straight out of the South, landing on the elite shores of two of America's most exclusive schools, Choate and Yale.

Inevitably, the experience changed me, broadened my horizons, and gave me a taste of Ivy League living. I was bright enough to feed off it, but not bold enough to grab hold of what this piece of good fortune had offered me. I allowed that tide to suck me back down to Columbus, Georgia, and accept a job with LeGrand, who was running the family jewelry business. It was an insular, constricting, timeless world of limited opportunity. There was nothing wrong with it if your ambitions were small. But mine were not.

I could have returned to the family home in Florence, Alabama, a smaller version of Columbus that had absolutely nothing to do with its Italian namesake. But that would not have worked either. I should have remained where my education had taken me and joined my Yale classmates on Wall Street or some other avenue that led to the great big world of opportunity.

So I had to do it the hard way, bit by bit, mistake by mistake, until I established myself in the world of real estate with some years of pretty high-flying success.

Now, as I approach my seventy-eighth birthday, I thought it was time to follow the advice of several friends and put this story down in writing, not just for my own satisfaction or to satisfy my family's curiosity, but also in the hope that readers may benefit from some hints on how to pick one's way through life's ever-challenging minefield. When I was growing up, Fred Astaire was singing that song, "Pick yourself up, dust yourself off and start all over again."

I did that a few times and, on occasion, had a lot of excitement along the way, through three children and four marriages and some fun times on the polo field and tennis court. Not to mention playing my trumpet in a Dixieland band.

Whatever trumpet playing I do in these pages will be tempered by the false notes which, I suppose, are all part of life's rich pattern. It has been quite a ride. But let me start at the beginning.

THE EARLY YEARS

I was born in Atlanta, Georgia, on November 29, 1936. My family lived in College Park, a suburb of Atlanta. Dad ran a jewelry store downtown. He and his brothers owned a chain of "Tiffany"-type stores in the southeastern United States. My earliest recollections are of the latter years of World War II, when there was some rationing of goods and the news of the day was the newsreel at the local theatre, showing grainy black and white footage of the post invasion operations in Europe and the brutal beach landings in the Pacific. How totally unlike the 24/7 news cycle of today.

The war was far removed from the everyday events of life in Georgia, but occasionally it came a bit closer to home. One of my older cousins, Hunley Elebash, was a Marine stationed in Atlanta for training. He and two of his fellow Marines would often come to our home in the "country" for Sunday lunch and a bit of R&R. As far as I was concerned, the "Three Marines" were there for my entertainment. They helped me with paper airplanes, made simply by folding 8½" x 11" paper into something that might stay aloft for twenty yards, more or less. My older friends in the neighborhood were more adept than I was at this sport, so the Marines were the great equalizer. After all, they had engineering backgrounds which trumped my friends' more rudimentary skills.

But I soon discovered I had a more interesting talent. Cousin Hunley, who was to play an influential part in my life, gave me the aforementioned trumpet which I quickly learned to play to a reasonable standard. It turned out to be the instrument that would pay my way through college when I got to Yale in 1955, allowing me to broaden my horizons and gain entry to the stimulating jazz world of New York City.

We lived in College Park until my father and his brothers lost their lease on the building they occupied in downtown Atlanta. They had a small part of a large building, and it was being demolished to make space for a much larger building, I think it may have been a Rich's department store. Anyway, it meant we would be moving, and the interim destination was to be Pensacola, Florida. This was "temporary unemployment" for my father, as he and his oldest brother, LeGrand, sought another location in another town. We had vacationed in Pensacola for many years, as it was my mother's hometown. Several of her sisters lived there, but the one I knew best was Jesse, mother of Wilmer (a boy), Charlie, and Janie. We were summer friends from previous vacations, and I was greatly enamored of my slightly older cousins. They lived in an old house, circa 1900, with a view over Pensacola Bay. Very rustic, but fascinating—there was a two-hundred-year-old oak tree in the backyard, and Wilmer and his older brother, Charlie, would play "tag" in the tree. They could literally run around on the branches, at various heights, avoiding being tagged. Janie was a beauty, and had a boyfriend, Lawrence Scott, who soon would be the captain of the University of Florida football team. Wilmer, Lawrence, and I would go to the high school gym and play basketball. They were pretty good, and a few years older. Good fun, and good experience for me.

I had another friend who lived just down the street from Wilmer's family. "Red" Fischer had a motorbike. I desperately wanted to ride it at every opportunity, and Red was very generous in giving me rights to the bike. My father expressly forbade me riding, but he often caught me just by driving through the neighborhood. I was like a recalcitrant puppy, very sorry to get caught, but not about to pass up the opportunity.

We lived across the bay bridge, in a cottage on the bay side of Santa Rosa Island. The bay beach was my front yard. Wilmer and I would fish, net crabs, and spear flounders, plus we sometimes had a small skiff available, equipped with an Evinrude outboard motor that would absolutely fly. My sister, Margaret Ann, was married to a Pensacola boy, Dicky Baker, and he was a terrific coach in all matters to do with enjoying water sports. He would take me fishing in the Gulf of Mexico for pompano. At the time, this was a stealth operation. First, catch the bait, which was sand crabs that came to the beach on every wave, then immediately burrowed down in the sand. When you saw one, you rushed to the spot and scooped up as much sand as possible and pitched it away from the water. About every third attempt, you would send a sand crab up onto dry land, and catch it. Using white line, silver hook, and leader, you would carefully place the hook through the sand crab, cast it out about twenty yards into the gulf, and then quickly retreat to a point ten yards away from the water's edge and lie down on the sand. If the pompano could see you on the beach, they would not take the bait.

Too much trouble, you say, but pompano were not sold in the market, and they were a delicacy. Today, I buy my pompano at a Publix supermarket.

Adapting to a new school was a snap. This new school was, by grade level, about a year behind the school I left in College Park. So, I could concentrate on my social life (such as it was at that age) and my fun experiences on the beach.

Soon thereafter, the family bought a jewelry store in Florence, Alabama. Dad was to be the manager, so we drove north to the northwest corner of Alabama, about twenty-five miles east of Mississippi and eighteen miles south of Tennessee. Today, the area is known as Muscle Shoals. I distinctly remember driving into town on the main street, and it appeared to be unpaved. Actually, it was just being resurfaced. We moved into a very modest house. I unpacked my bike and took off to see who lived in the neighborhood. The first kid I encountered was Dick Goodsell, who would become one of my best friends. His father owned the Ford tractor dealership, and Dick (AKA Mouse) was an expert at operating a tractor. He made money at a young age by moving the necessary dirt to contour yards for landscapers.

Through him, I immediately made friends—Johnny Archer, Don Patterson, Sonny Thompson, Fitz Hill, and Jimmy Thompson was the core group. We became the BSFH gang—that is, Brown Service Funeral Home, Johnny's family business. It was a big house, with the business operation on the ground floor, and the family residence upstairs. The head undertaker, Stanley, was tolerant of us hanging around, except when a "customer" was delivered, and then he wanted us to get lost. There was a basketball hoop in the backyard, nailed to a tree, and we played continuous games of "horse." I think this helped me when it came to playing on the high school team. We also played cards upstairs on occasion. We spent most of our spare time at Brown Service, and we were never much concerned about the business on the first floor. I played in the school band and orchestra, continually improving my skill with the trumpet. It was the early '50s, and the Korean War was underway. At our age, it was not on our front burner, but I began to notice it when I was called by the American Legion to play taps at military funerals.

To make money, I sold newspapers on the street and to a select group of customers in the business establishments on Main Street. Then, I would go to the bus terminal and sell more papers to the workers going home out in the countryside. Eventually, this provided me with my very own Whizzer motorbike. I eventually found more work, playing in a small dance music group, at the VFW club on Saturday nights. What I remember most vividly about that experience was once drinking several bourbon and Coca-Cola highballs, which made me violently ill. It would be many years before I could even look at a bottle of bourbon.

As a typical high school junior in 1953, I was playing in the school band and was a starter on the Coffee High School basketball team. But my friends, mostly seniors, were headed to the University of Alabama or, in some cases, Auburn, the following year.

OPPORTUNITY KNOCKS

However, fate decreed that I would not join them. One day, LeGrand Elebash Jr. showed up. LeGrand was chief executive of the family business and carried himself as such. He was, to say the least, an impressive character. His own father, "Big LeGrand," was the oldest of six children and had started the business after dropping out of school at about the sixth grade level. His parents had migrated to Selma, Alabama, from Rochester, New York, some time after the Civil War ended. He had experienced the hard scrabble world of the post-war south, but, as the jewelry business prospered, he saw the opportunity of affording his two sons, LeGrand and Shearen, the kind of education he had never enjoyed. The best that the country had to offer. So he sent them both to Choate School in Wallingford, Connecticut, and then to Yale.

"Big" never learned to drive a car, but he had an appreciation of the finer things of life. Like others of that period, he emulated the Robber Barons in many ways—developing a taste for fine furniture, silver, art, and classical music. I don't think I ever saw him without a necktie and a stiff collar until his health failed and he started to go downhill fast with cancer in 1960.

When I met his son LeGrand in 1953, he looked like the genuine product of an Ivy League education. He dressed like an Englishman and had travelled the world. He was friends with many of the offspring of the Robber Barons who filled the ranks at Yale, Harvard, and Princeton in that era. It was all very impressive for a high school junior from north Alabama who had never been north of Bristol, Virginia.

LeGrand had no children of his own, and, perhaps eyeing me as a surrogate son, he took an immediate interest in me. To our surprise, he offered to send me to Choate. He was an excellent salesman and backed up his suggestion with Choate's school catalogue, showing photographs of boys in tweed jackets, charcoal pants, button-down shirts, and stripe neckties. The magnificent buildings, donated by people with names like Mellon, and sports about which I knew absolutely nothing—soccer, rowing, and lacrosse—were intimidating but exciting. Although my parents had misgivings about this proposed adventure, I was sold.

So, one hot and memorable day in August 1953, I boarded a train in Birmingham for New York City, where I would change trains for Wallingford. My seat was in coach so there was no bed. I was carrying two big suitcases which held all of my prep school clothes. The train pulled out of Birmingham at 5:00 p.m. and my life-changing journey had begun.

The next morning, I watched the Virginia countryside flash by, and by midafternoon, we were pulling into

Penn Station, the end of the line for this train. For a country boy from the quiet south, the cacophony and chaos of one of New York City's great terminals was just the beginning of my culture shock. How I made it across town to Grand Central I have no idea. It was a good thing that I was already a strongly built young man because two large suitcases did not make it an easy journey. But, after gaping at Grand Central's great marble halls and broad staircases, I made the train for Wallingford and settled back in eager anticipation of what lay ahead.

As we pulled into Wallingford, I could see the welcoming committee on the platform, teachers and administrators with signs identifying them as greeters for Choate students. After a short bus ride, we were on the campus I had seen in the catalogue. The first order of business was to go to your assigned house, find your room, and meet your roommate. Mine turned out to be a nice guy from Tulsa, Oklahoma. He was a returning student so all this was old hat to him. He greeted me warmly, which helped put me somewhat at ease. After unpacking, he said, "Let's go out on the hall and I will introduce you to some of the guys who live on this floor."

"Great," I responded eagerly.

The first person he corralled was another old boy from Meriden, Connecticut.

"Eddie," he said. "I want you to meet my new room-mate, Pete Elebash. He's from Alabama."

I extended my hand and said, "Hi, Eddie!"

Eddie looked me in the eye and said, "Oh no, not another damn Southerner!"

I was left standing there, not knowing how to react. All I could think was that if this was typical of Choate, my new life was not going to be very pleasant.

Classes started the next day. Our assignments and course schedules were in our mailbox, a cubbyhole along a wall on the ground floor. When I looked at the daily assignments for the first week, I thought there must be a mistake. The first WEEK? Surely this must be for the first MONTH!

The first semester was terrible for me. I was not prepared for the workload which far exceeded anything I had been used to and I was fearful of flunking out and going home with my tail between my legs. Nobody was particularly friendly either, and I slept very little. I was struggling to keep up in class, and for the first time in my life, I prayed daily to God for help. How embarrassing if I let LeGrand down, after he had paid my tuition and paid for all of my clothes. I had never known failure thus far in my life and this situation was grave.

Fall sports started and everybody was cheering our boys on in football, soccer, and cross country against schools named Deerfield, Kent, Hotchkiss, and Taft. Fortunately, I did not have a fall sport which allowed me more time to study. It also meant that no one was paying any attention to this new boy from Alabama. Just like Br'er Rabbit, I was lying low. I was gradually making the adjustment from an Alabama high school to one of the most highly regarded prep schools in the country. But the learning curve was steep. I had to deal with five subjects and read fifty pages of History and

English per day. Luckily, I was good at math, which eased the burden a bit.

When the winter sports tryouts were announced, I stuck my head above the parapet for the first time and went out for basketball. Back home, I had dreamed of going on to play for the University of Alabama. Here, I was not at all sure I would even make the team. Until the first practice session. To my surprise, it became immediately clear to me and my teammates that I was the best basketball player at Choate!

"Why didn't you tell us you were so good at b'ball?" they asked. "We haven't seen or heard from you since the school year started."

"Nobody asked me," I replied.

Well, from that moment on, my life at Choate took on a very different hue. Suddenly, I was popular and people were saying how modest I was. Not true, of course. I had just been plain scared like a fish out of water.

But now I was swimming with the tide, riding the wave, fulfilling the promise I had shown in that first practice by becoming the high scorer on the team. Academically, things were looking up too. I was finally on track to pass my courses and life up north was becoming a very different, happier experience. I was elected captain of the team for the next year and my parents were loving the news articles on our team that were being sent to the Florence newspaper.

In the spring, I tried out for the golf team. This time, I wasn't the best but it was close. It was a tossup between me and two brothers from Texas. I played the number-one slot so I was always playing the opposition's best player. Yet I only lost one match—to the Yale freshman named Peter Nisselson, one up in nineteen holes. He went on to win the Bermuda Open that year so I wasn't too disappointed with that one loss.

More importantly, perhaps, I was sailing along near the top in all my classes. What a change from those dark days in September. I now had many friends and a small group of us had become student leaders for our class. I was to be the incoming Chairman of the Honor Committee, a member of the Student Council, and President of the Athletic Association. The latter position was a job that mainly consisted of being the MC at the three athletic banquets that were held after each sports season ended. No more laying low for Elebash. Suddenly, I was up front, center, and very visible.

On top of everything else, I was keeping up with my music. I played in the school orchestra as well occasionally with a little jazz group. What a year it had become. Looking back, I can say with confidence that my first year at Choate was the most formative experience of my life. The motto was work hard, be of good character, truthful, and considerate of others. If you were not willing to live by that motto, you would be sent packing. The Headmaster, Seymour St. John, along with others like George Steele and Stanley Pratt, were an inspiration to us as well as decades of Choate students.

COLUMBUS, GEORGIA

The year had opened my eyes and I returned south in the summer of 1954 as a different and more confident person. I had seen a new world and I liked it. I owed it all, of course, to LeGrand, and it was to my great benefactor that I returned in Columbus, Georgia, rather than to my parents in Florence. LeGrand and his wife Lucy had no children and I began to realize that I was the "missing link," at least for LeGrand. He now had a "son" who had come through the schoolboy equivalent of the Navy Seal's famous BUD/S course where only about 30 percent of those enrolled move on to the next level. I viewed it as a great opportunity and quickly put my complete trust in LeGrand to shape my future.

Columbus was, and remains, a very nice southern city, filled with friendly people the likes of which I had known in Florence. But it was much larger. The 1950s was, in many ways, the golden age of the USA, particularly in the south. The end of WWII had brought a wave of prosperity to the region and there were no imminent foreign threats to our lifestyle. In contrast to what followed, it was a gentle era—Frank Sinatra, Rosemary Clooney, and Doris Day sang the hit songs;

kids hung out at the local soda fountain while President Eisenhower, good old war hero Ike, signed into law the interstate highway program, without which America might have come to a grinding halt.

Down in the south, we were relatively immune from the warning signs, flagged by Hollywood and Broadway, of how the world was going to change. In 1955, James Dean made his huge, short-lived impact with *Rebel Without a Cause* while that same year, nationwide audiences were offered a shocking insight into public school life in New York City when Sydney Poitier starred in *The Blackboard Jungle* with its accompanying hit tune "Rock Around the Clock." Bill Haley and his Comets were heralding the birth of rock 'n' roll, and the music world would never be the same again.

And, after the romance and comparative gentility of *Oklahoma!* and *The Sound of Music*, Broadway pointed the way to a tougher, edgier form of entertainment with *West Side Story*. A musical about Puerto Ricans in New York? It was all too far removed from our cosseted, traditional world in the Deep South, and even when I returned to Choate, there might as well have been an ocean between us and the problems Poitier depicted in *The Blackboard Jungle*.

In Columbus that first summer, I socialized mostly with LeGrand and Lucy's friends, a much older group, while also making some friends of my own age. They were, largely, lawyers in training, or boys from families who owned local businesses which offered them good future prospects. It soon became obvious to me that my cousin had, in his mind and by most secular measurements, far outstripped his circle of friends, mainly because of the contacts he had made at Yale. They were, for want of a better description, the offspring of the old-line families of the nineteenth century. He was fascinated by their lifestyle. Most of these people had become immensely wealthy before 1900 and lived accordingly—Park Avenue apartments, all the right clubs, shooting syndicates in England, and quail plantations in the south. The walls of their homes dripped with French impressionists and old masters and, when you visited, uniformed butlers and maids tended to your every need. One must remember, of course, that a large portion of their family fortunes were accumulated before income taxes were collected. None of this, I hasten to add, prevented them from being very charming and pleasant people to be around. It was just that they lived by a totally different standard than the rest of the country at that time.

So I fitted into LeGrand's world as best I could, impressed by how he went about things and regretful in later years that I had not been more insightful about everything going on in his world, for better or for worse, and how that would affect me in later life.

My sixth form year at Choate was, in many respects, as rewarding a period of my life as I have ever enjoyed. I was one of three sixth formers who, to a great extent, were running student affairs and serving as advisers to the Headmaster. I will never forget that year with Jeremy Packard, Peter Seed, and myself being entrusted with so much responsibility. We could not have received a better education anywhere than we did that year as student leaders with tremendous support from the entire faculty and Headmaster Seymour St. John. Fifty years later, I had the pleasure of hosting Seymour and his wife at the International Tennis Hall of Fame tennis tournament at Newport, Rhode Island. He died shortly thereafter. Seymour will always be remembered as an outstanding Headmaster for everyone who attended Choate during his time.

As graduation neared, we all began to contemplate our next destination. Unlike today, we pretty much had our choice of the best Ivy League colleges. Since my cousin and his brother had gone to Yale, I was naturally leaning that way. I did take a Princeton application, but when I realized it was two pages longer than Yale's, I tossed it in the trash. Can you imagine anyone doing that today?

I returned to Columbus for the summer, a little bit wiser, a little bit more confident, and eagerly awaiting the greater freedom college would bring me after Choate. At Yale, there would be little or no adult supervision. You were supposed to stand on your own two feet and plot your own path in life.

YALE

So it was that, in the fall of 1955, I began four years at Yale which, for this young man from Alabama, was an extraordinary experience. I soon realized that I was being afforded the best education you could find anywhere in the world. American studies had just been added as a major, so mine was one of the first classes to graduate from this program. Because it was new, our teachers were selected from other majors—history, philosophy, literature, political science, and history of art. They were the very best in their field. John Blum and Edmund Morgan in history, Brad Westerfield in political science, and Vincent Scully in history of art were brilliant and have long been regarded as among the best ever at Yale.

Many of my classmates joined the ROTC and I chose the Army. Fortunately for me, after freshman year, I was able to escape the dining room work assignment and become a student aide to the ROTC office. All scholarship students were required to hold a job on campus all four years. The ROTC office was a good fit for me as I was interested in things military and I enjoyed interacting with the military staff, especially, the history professor who taught the required military history course. "Wild Bill" Emerson was one of my absolute favorite Yale professors, bringing to life military conflicts of old as well as WWII. In my senior year, I was appointed Commander of the Cadet Corps, which was mostly a parade ground position at the head of the formation. But it kept me in close touch with the staff.

In my sophomore year, I joined the DKE fraternity. Back then, the frat houses were essentially country clubs without golf, tennis, or swimming facilities. I pledged DKE, along with a few friends, mainly because it was known as the "jock house," and I was on the freshman basketball team. Many of the brothers were football, basketball, or hockey players. Each fraternity had its signature feature—Fence Club was mostly New York social types, plus some hockey players. There were two more fraternities operating back then, whose Greek names I cannot recall. One was predominately midwestern guys and the other was more academically inclined. The initiation ceremony was brutal. We pledges were spanked with big wooden paddles and made to eat some awful things. It was very unpleasant, and I thought way over the top. The next year when I was a member and pledge initiation rolled around, I tried to get our members to tone it down. Most agreed with me, but some insisted of roughing up the pledges simply because it had been done to them.

Once that was over, we settled into a very civilized mode, drinking, playing pool, and taking some meals at the house. Everyone lived in a residential college—I was in Berkeley—but we partied at the DKE house.

From time to time, fraternity members would visit other houses, particularly if one house was having a big party on the weekend. We often had bands playing on Saturday night. Lots of the members would have dates come down from Smith, Wellesley, Vassar, and Bennett Junior College. The girls stayed in the local hotels and would arrive in time for the football game at the Yale Bowl. After the game, it was back to the frat house and the party continued long into the night. Most of us were drinking beer or liquor, but not too many got drunk. After all, if you overimbibed, you were not likely to enjoy any private time with your date! Yale was not co-ed then, so the rare opportunity to smell perfume instead of liniment in the locker room was important enough to stay sober. Many of my friends would drive to a girlfriend's college for a weekend, but I was pretty booked up with my Dixie band until my senior year so that was a rare event for me. Only once did I have a date come to Yale when I was playing in the band. The young lady did not realize that she would be sitting by the band stand all night. She was not amused!

In later years, the fraternities were moved, or, one might say, kicked off campus and became less of a factor in the undergraduate lifestyle.

In the spring of junior year, the senior societies tapped a group of fifteen rising seniors to become members for the coming year. Back then, there were six such societies, fifteen men each, who met twice a week at their tombs (as the buildings were called). All members were sworn to secrecy and were not allowed to greet or speak with a nonmember walking to and from meetings, which were held on Thursday and Sunday evenings. I believe the point of this was to avoid disclosing any information about what was said and done inside, as personal information about members was often a topic of discussion. I was fortunate to be tapped by Book & Snake and this experience with fourteen talented classmates, some of whom I did not meet until we were "initiated," was extremely rewarding. Today, there are many new societies, most composed of eight men and eight women, and some are not as secretive as in the old days.

In the meantime, my musical interest had blossomed after hearing Dixieland music played by some of the best in the business. Immediately after checking into the freshman campus at Yale, I ran into a fellow enthusiast, Michael Mallory, who had a Dixie band at the Hill School with none other than Fred Waring Jr., an excellent trombonist. Michael and I set about rounding up a band at Yale. I played trumpet and Michael played the guitar, but we needed a piano, clarinet, trombone, drummer, and bass to create the sound we wanted. The first iteration of the "Yale Bullpups," as we were known, was not exactly ready for prime time, but it was a start. Quickly we began to cull, looking for the best musicians, regardless of their Yale connection. As luck would have it, we found another Yale undergraduate, who was an unbelievably good piano player, Chuck Folds, who could play any style, and he loved Dixie. We found an excellent trombone player at the Yale Law School, Hank Bredenberg, who is still playing in south Florida with touring bands, and an extraordinary clarinet man, Brad Terry, who had studied under Benny Goodman. He was our age but not in school and we were happy to have him. In addition, we found a succession of drummers and bass men from the New Haven area. The sound was good and we quickly became popular, so much so that we actually got paid to perform at fraternity houses on weekends.

There was a roadhouse near Millbrook, New York, just east of Poughkeepsie, owned by an old Dixie trumpet man, who would let us play for the college boys coming from near and far to visit the girls at Bennett Junior College and Vassar. No pay, but all you could eat and drink. It was the perfect place to hone our skills and broaden our repertoire. I vividly remember the night that I noticed, from the bandstand, a strikingly beautiful blond, wearing a white turtleneck angora sweater and a short, painted-on black skirt. She was dancing by herself and had incredibly seductive moves.

"Who is that girl?" I inquired.

"That is Jane Fonda, a student at Vassar," I was told by another student. I introduced myself, and asked if I could take her to dinner some night. She answered in the affirmative, and so I drove up to Vassar on a week night for that express purpose. We had a cordial dinner, but I realized that this was way more horse than I could handle. From time to time, I saw her at parties at the Fence Club, in the company of one of the wealthier, more sophisticated upperclassmen.

Soon we were making frequent trips into New York City to visit legendary jazz venues like Eddie Condon's, Jimmy Ryan's, and the Metropole. Michael had an MG, and we would drive into New York City after dinner, catch at least two shows at two different clubs then drive back to New Haven in time to get maybe four hours' sleep before classes the next day. We began to make friends with some of the jazz groups, and we were continually adding new material to our song book. Traffic back then was not a problem, so we could make the one-way trip in less than two hours. We were learning fast and it became clear to me that this dog would hunt.

After our freshman year, I sent out a mass mailing to every prep school, fraternity, and sorority within a two-hundred-mile radius of New Haven. The response was, to put it mildly, overwhelming. Now, for me, the rubber was going to hit the road. Decisions had to be made. Freshman year, I had played basketball. The competition was several levels above the prep school league but I was a starter and slated to be either fifth or sixth man on the varsity the following year. In addition to the band and basketball, I had the scholarship job in the freshman dining room, although, as I have said, I was about to be upgraded to student assistant in the Army ROTC office. Something was going to have to go. I had to choose between basketball and the band. I did not have the money to enjoy Yale's social life and the band was becoming a money machine for me. And, frankly, I was burnt out with team sports. Being honest with myself, I knew I was not going to be an all Ivy player and I could live a good life, with money to spare, if I dropped off the team. It was an easy choice for me at the time.

I grabbed every opportunity to slip into Manhattan and mix with the jazz crowd, befriending some of the old Basie and Ellington musicians who were living and playing around the city. We even managed to get them to play with us at some special events. In return, they would take me to some of their clubs and this southern boy suddenly found himself deep in Harlem, being taken care of by the likes of Buddy Tate, one of the all-time great sax men. I met and played with Buck Clayton, Roy Eldridge, and Rex Stewart, all famous trumpet men. We were even allowed to play intermission at Condon's, which, at the time, had, in my opinion, the best Dixie front line ever—Edmund Hall on clarinet, Wild Bill Davison on coronet, and Cutty Cutshall on trombone.

Through our clarinetist, Brad Terry, we were invited to bring the band to Benny Goodman's home in Stamford, Connecticut. At sometime in the past, Brad had been a student of the "King of Swing," hence the introduction. Needless to say, we were thrilled at the prospect of meeting Goodman and playing in his presence. He had a recording studio in his home, and after we set up, he asked us to play one of our favorite songs. I picked "Back Home Again in Indiana," a staple of the Dixie world at that time.

After greeting us cordially, he barely said a word once he started recording, and was fully occupied with his recording equipment. At his request, we played this song over and over and over, as he kept fiddling with the dials. At some point, he picked up his clarinet and played with us. We were ecstatic to have the great man actually in our front line, and, boy, could he play. Of course, we had heard him on records, but in person, close up, this was the experience of a lifetime.

We were with him for about three hours, as he made numerous tapes of that same song. Stupidly, I never asked him for one of the tapes but, for us, the memory of the event was priceless.

The Goodman episode was, for us, historic. Two other adventures come to mind, both being humorous and hazardous. Many of our jobs were north of New Haven, and the Interstate Highway network was not yet built. So, in the dead of winter, driving on secondary roads in a snowstorm was not for the faint of heart. The Taconic State Parkway did exist but was plowed infrequently. Very hazardous conditions, to say the least. Our old Ford station wagon did not have snow tires, so there was much sliding about as we attempted to stay on the road.

This was the scene as we headed out to RPI in Troy, New York, for a Saturday night performance at a frat house. We had the street address, but no GPS in those days, so when we finally arrived in Troy, the next challenge was to find the frat house. It was blizzard conditions and the streets were completely buried under the snow. We hailed down a lone pedestrian, and asked for directions.

"Sure" he said. "At the next light, take a left, then an immediate left at the next street. The house is about two blocks down on the right."

The first turn was good, but the second turn was a disaster: instead of a street, we were on the railroad tracks! In the snowstorm we could not distinguish the tracks from a street, so we were stuck. Some good citizen of Troy ran out to us, saying, "You can't stop there—the train comes in about fifteen minutes!" Well, you have heard of superhuman strength exhibited by ordinary people when their life is threatened: we all pushed like mad to extricate ourselves from the tracks. Shortly we found our job site and the dear brothers were happy to see us even if we were two hours late.

The third episode occurred when we drove to Hamilton, New York, in the snow, to play at a frat house at Colgate. We arrived on time, began setting up and tuning our instruments to the piano, a nice look-ing baby grand. We suddenly discovered that the piano was so badly out of tune that we could not adjust our instruments to it. I began to panic, because this could potentially be a disaster. Chuck Folds, our super-tal-ented piano man, saved the day.

"Don't worry, guys, I will just transpose every tune up one-half a tone."

This meant that, if the song was written to be played in the key of C, Chuck would need to, on the fly, play it in C sharp. If you are not a musician, ask someone who is how hard that would be. The answer would be "virtually impossible."

The party was really hopping as the evening pro-ceeded, and the booze was flowing, when the drummer pointed to the floor under the piano. I looked to see what he was trying to say, and there, under the piano, was a wasted frat boy with a big kitchen knife trying to carve the front leg off the piano! Fortunately he was not having much success, but was doing serious damage to a perfectly good—but out of tune—piano. Some of his friends dragged him away, all laughing at his prank.

It is a wonder that we all survived to tell these stories. Life for a road musician is not for sissies, and by my senior year, I was ready to relinquish my trumpet seat to one of the real pros with whom we had become friends. Business was good, and some nights I would book two jobs, and fill the ranks from our stable of talent around New York. Finally, I could attend a party at Yale with a date instead of my trumpet. I decided that I would give up playing, and actually gave my horn to a friend, Jim Trowbridge, one of Gene Scott's roommates, who was eager to play. More about Gene Scott later, but he was perhaps one of the most talented athletes to ever attend Yale. He earned four varsity letters every year. How, you ask, as there are only three sports seasons? He was captain of the soccer team, first string on the hockey team, and played one of the top three slots on the tennis team. He was the most talented tennis player, but the distraction of the other sports meant one of the other fellows was a bit sharper in the spring. Both Gene and one of his teammates, Donald Dell, went on to great heights in the world of tennis. So, the fourth letter came from winning the high jump in Yale track meets, whenever the tennis schedule allowed.

After I had completed my exams and was killing time before graduation, I decided to go watch the Yale-Princeton tennis match. I had never been interested in playing tennis, but Gene was a good friend, and we lived in the same residential college, Berkeley. The match was an eye opener for me—this looked like a great sport for after college, fast and athletic, not sedentary like golf. Later I told Gene I thought I would try my hand at tennis after graduation. He presented me with one of his racquets, an old Wilson Kramer (it was as heavy as an ax!). He said, "Go hit a ball against a backboard, and look for guys who know how to play. Watch them, and monkey see, monkey do." A year later, I was doing exactly as he instructed.

At a time when tuition, room, and board at Yale was $2000 per annum, I was pocketing a fair stack of money and still enjoying a nice social life. Ever since sophomore year, I was able to be financially independent. LeGrand was shocked when I told him he would not need to continue paying tuition, room, and board.

PALM BEACH

Michael Mallory's family had a winter home in Palm Beach and they very kindly invited me down for the spring vacation. Palm Beach is about as far from Florence, Alabama, as it is from Mars.

Palm Beach in 1956 was unlike anything I had ever seen, but it was still very low-key compared to today. It was exclusively a winter watering hole for the upper class of that era. It was all old money and no entrepreneurs. No Bill Gates, Warren Buffets, or Steve Jobs, just old families who had built America's great industrial complex in the early twentieth century. There was, to say the least, a rather rigid social structure, but youngsters like me, from good schools, were welcomed. For the week that I was enjoying this splendor, the daily routine was not too hard to take. It was off to the Bath & Tennis Club in the morning for tennis followed by the beach and lunch. Then to the Everglades Club for golf, followed by cocktails on the patio, listening to the Meyer Davis Trio playing background music while we planned the evening's activities. Most nights there was a party somewhere, usually black tie, and with no shortage of girls attending, it was always interesting.

For those of you who know the area, the amount to which it has changed can be gauged by the fact that, in 1956, Military Trail was a dirt road with nothing paved to the west of it. The City of West Palm Beach was basically a slum district, not to be visited after dark. So we stuck to our part of town. Several years later, we brought our band down on a spring vacation road trip and were able to secure a few paying jobs in Fort Lauderdale and Miami. We also made ourselves known in Palm Beach, putting on an impromptu performance in a private home, much to the chagrin of the man of the house. But that's what can happen when you have young daughters.

On the way down to Palm Beach, we stopped in Atlanta where we were hired to play at the Piedmont Driving Club, which was one of the few private clubs with a real ballroom. It was cavernous and, to our surprise, it was packed, standing room only. They had more reservations for the night we played than for any other function that year. Reacting to a big, enthusiastic crowd, we blew the roof off the place. We mixed up the song selection to accommodate a slightly older audience than we normally faced, with some songs from the Cole Porter songbook. It obviously went down well because we were asked to stay an extra night, good pay check, full room and board, and I had no hesitation in accepting the offer, especially as our old Ford station wagon had run out of steam and was in the shop. I cannot recall the name of the member who hired us, but he invited all of his Atlanta friends to the party at his home. The next morning, we retrieved our wagon, paid the repair bill with our "bonus money," and departed for Palm Beach.

As graduation approached, career decisions became a matter of concern to all of us. I wish I had considered all the options and thought about it a little more. Instead, I made a decision that, in retrospect, I consider the worst mistake of my life. I went back to Columbus and joined cousin LeGrand in business. Just what kind of business was far from clear at the time, but I just assumed it would work out. Not clever. I will explain in greater detail as the story unfolds.

THE ARMY: FORT BENNING, GEORGIA

In the meantime, I had to satisfy my active duty obligation to the US Army. Having selected infantry as my branch of service, I received orders to report to Fort Benning, Georgia, in September. The first order of business was to complete the Basic Officers Training Course. We were all officers, but needed to learn leadership and combat skills. The ten-week course was a highly regimented, no-nonsense program run by seasoned noncommissioned officers who had a pretty direct way of letting you know if you were not pulling your weight. There was also classroom work, but we were mostly in the field, learning land navigation (at night in the woods or swamp), small arms or mortars (indirect fire requiring math calculations), hand-to-hand combat, and lots of "PT." This, of course, entailed running until you could no longer stand and lots of pushups and pullups, all designed to get us fighting fit. We were also schooled in small-unit tactics and platoon-sized operations. We were a gung-ho bunch, all volunteers, and nobody quit. When we graduated, I was astonished to receive a small piece of photocopied paper, telling me that I was the honor graduate of our class with the highest combined scores. This was news to the ROTC department at Yale and congratulations began to hit my mailbox. It was a nice way to begin a brief career in the military.

All of us newly trained officers were offered a selection of assignments. It was our choice and I chose parachute training. All through the Basic Officers Course, I had been running past the 250-foot jump towers which were across the street from our assembly point. I thought it would be cool to have jump wings on my uniform, so I signed up for the four-week airborne school. It was physically challenging, quite apart from testing our courage. First, it was the thirty-four-foot towers. We stood in a doorway about three stories high and jumped, falling about ten feet until the slack was gone from our harness and we slid down a cable on a pulley to the ground. There is something about being only thirty-four feet above the ground while talking to the instructor on the ground who is going to give the command "Go!" No one in their right mind would stand in the window on the third floor of an office building and jump. It was far more frightening than jumping from 1,200 feet because, up there, you were looking straight ahead, not down, and could not make out objects and people on the ground. Also the air blast from the plane's engines created the sensation of being swept along in a river, not falling as deadweight.

Next came the 250-foot towers, which resembled some rides at the fair. We put on a parachute that was fully opened with the canopy attached to a circular ring on a cable. We were hauled up to the top of the tower and released to float down to the ground. In other words, it was the last 250 feet of an actual jump. Very few of us were nearly as concerned about this as we were about the dreaded thirty-four-foot tower. When we went to the airplanes for the first jump, most of us were thinking to ourselves, "Why are we going to jump out of perfectly good airplanes?"

However, once the parachutes opened, the fear left us and we were talking in the air and were still babbling about the experience when we hit the drop zone. Five jumps and we were done with this school and I thought I would never jump out of a plane again. How wrong I was.

The next assignment was to go to a rifle company training raw recruits. This was deadly dull work so I was delighted that Army policy had changed and that reserve officers with a six-month active duty commitment were being released early. Our requirement was to join a reserve unit somewhere, with monthly meetings and two weeks of summer camp. But basically it meant that I was done with the military, or so I thought. In 1959, the world was at peace and the armed services were cutting back everywhere. Within two years, everything had changed. Trouble in Berlin, Lebanon, and Vietnam reversed the cut-back policy. Suddenly, reserve officers like me were being called back to active duty. A friend of mine in Columbus in my same situation was reactivated even though he was married with children. If they wanted him, I realized I could not be far behind.

THE GREEN BERETS

As I contemplated my situation, I decided that I absolutely must find a unit made up of well-trained, highly qualified people. I had a fear of being called back and assigned to a rifle company of novices who couldn't shoot straight. As I was stewing over this, I received a call one night at 9:00 p.m. from Don Patterson, an old friend from Florence, who was an attorney. I asked him what he was doing in Columbus and he replied, "I am at Fort Benning in the officers' club with a group of reservists from the Alabama National Guard and we are at the airborne school."

Don told me about the 20th Special Forces Group, part of a network of SF units on the east coast of the US. My heart leaped to my throat. "Where do you meet?" I asked, trying to control my enthusiasm. "Do you need any officers who already have jump wings?" As luck would have it, the answer was yes and, even better, his commanding officer was right there with him and said he would be delighted to interview me. I ran to my car and made the twenty-minute drive to Ft. Benning in less than fifteen. Two drinks later, I signed up. If I had to go back on active duty, at least I would be with a top flight group. Meanwhile, I would attend meetings in Alexander City, Alabama, less than a two-hour drive from my home in Columbus.

The training with the 20th SF Group was interesting and intense. Almost every weekend, our A-team, consisting of twelve men, would simulate a typical SF assignment, jumping behind enemy lines and meeting up with rebels, organizing, training, and supplying them to overthrow a dictator. The original Special Forces concept was patterned on the OSS in WWII operating in France. I had seen movies about it. Those OSS teams and the civilians they organized played a major role in running the Nazis out of the occupied countries of Western Europe. We were training with world hotspots in mind—the Middle East, some Caribbean islands, Europe, be it jungle, desert, or mountainous terrain. Very soon the focus would be on Vietnam.

Living in Columbus near Ft. Benning made it easy for me to rack up practice jumps with students from the airborne school. Those training jumps were taken at an altitude of 1,200 feet on to a well-groomed drop zone. It was good for me to familiarize again with the necessary preparation and parachute gear. However, our A-team jumps were often at night, from an altitude of eight hundred feet on to an unimproved drop zone with about eighty pounds of equipment strapped on to our parachute harness by a twenty-five-foot drop line. A quick release allowed us to drop it just before we hit the ground. Our training included all kinds of explosives and small arms as well as learning how to bounce a radio transmission, in code, off the ionosphere so it could not be detected by the enemy between us and our base. In addition, we were taught how to deal with basic medical care for injuries and intelligence gathering. We played little war games, evading the enemy while spying on him, which is why the SF guys were sometimes referred to as "Sneaky Petes."

I was soon promoted to captain and given my own A-Team. These citizen soldiers were extremely good at what they were doing and well qualified in their specialty. I stayed with the 20th Special Forces until my time was up and I was discharged in 1967. We were fortunate not to be sent to Vietnam. I suppose it was all about timing. Under President Lyndon Johnson, Defense Secretary Robert McNamara, and General Westmoreland, the strategy was changed from a guerilla war to a full-scale operation with regular military units so the Special Forces mission was diminished. There were some SF units over there but our number never came up.

However, my time in the Army was not entirely peaceful or without incident. Training for foreign conflicts formed only part of our duties. There was trouble at home too. Integration issues were becoming front and center in the southern states.

GEORGE WALLACE'S
TROOPS

In 1954, the Supreme Court had ruled, in *Brown vs. Board of Education*, that the longstanding policy of "separate but equal" education in the United States was unconstitutional. This decision set southern states and their elected officials on a collision course with the US government. Governors like Lester Mattox in Georgia and George Wallace in Alabama won elections by promising never to yield to federal authority on this issue. On May 16, 1963, a federal court ordered that the University of Alabama, amongst others, must accept African American students immediately. Two students, Vivian Malone and James Hood, applied and Governor Wallace publicly declared he would "stand in the school house doorway" to prevent their enrollment.

It was a typical Sunday morning in Columbus, sun shining and birds singing, when my phone rang. On the other end, the duty officer at the 20th SF Group advised me that we were to report immediately (like before the sun went down) for duty at Tuscaloosa, Alabama. My instructions were handed down with that finite tone of military authority: move fast, do not disclose to anyone except your wife (I was not married at the time) where you are going, and be prepared to stay indefinitely.

That evening we were assembled at the armory in Tuscaloosa. Governor Wallace had mobilized us to control any civil unrest that might result from his intention to stand in the door on Tuesday morning when registration was to begin. This was not our typical mission so we set about practicing crowd control tactics we had seen used elsewhere. While doing so, we were stuck inside the armory for fear that the sight of the military would inflame tensions which were already close to the boiling point.

Monday was a day of typical military boredom for us. We were told to hurry up then wait. Then wait again. Nobody seemed to know what was going on, so we just cooled our heels in the armory. Later, we learned that negotiations were taking place between the governor's office and the White House in Washington. Not until Tuesday morning were we told that an agreement had been reached. Wallace would stand in the door and our commanding officer, General Graham and his staff, would approach the governor and say, words to the effect, "Governor, it is our sad duty to inform you that our National Guard troops have been federalized by President Kennedy so we are now federal troops whose orders are to remove you from the door and allow these two students to register for classes at the University of Alabama."

It was a moment of history for the United States of America. It was the turning of a page from which there was no turning back. It all took place as I have described with surprisingly little fuss. We were in formation on the street beside Foster Auditorium, at parade rest with rifles. If people assumed those rifles were loaded, they were wrong. We had no ammunition. There were very few witnesses to the strange scene that unfolded. Wallace, a small man with a countenance that suggested disapproval at the best of times, appeared in the doorway and was, in effect, told to go away by the troops he had summoned. Which he did. There were positions marked with chalk on the pavement for NBC, CBS, and ABC but there were few cameras and very little national press. Strangely, there was no national media covering a story that would affect the lives of children throughout the country. From Washington, Assistant Attorney General Nicholas Katzenbach was there, chatting with our troops and observing the ceremony unfolding at the door. There was no trouble or disturbance of any kind. Wallace had made a brief speech and removed himself from the doorway, allowing two brave young African Americans to enter. In about an hour's time, the whole thing was over and we were back in the armory.

As I thought about it later, I surmised that Wallace was allowed to say a few words, provided he accepted this moment as the end of his obstruction of federal law. He had honored his campaign pledge to resist for as long as possible. Most thinking people in the South had already accepted the fact that integration of the school systems, especially at the university level, was a foregone conclusion and that the best way forward was to simply accept the new reality. But, of course, it did not turn out to be that simple.

While our week at the armory in Tuscaloosa was punctuated by nothing more serious than a couple of false alarms over bomb threats etc, the situation was very different several years later. On August 6, 1965, with tensions rising to fever pitch as President Lyndon Johnson signed the Voting Rights Act into law, thousands set off on the historic Selma to Montgomery march. By then, the Civil Rights movement was in full swing, headed by Martin Luther King and personally backed by such high-profile figures as Harry Belafonte and Sydney Poitier. They were amongst eight thousand people who joined the march and the 20th SF was called out again—this time as part of a two-thousand-strong contingent of federal troops. And this time, the news organizations were there in force, recording every moment. People got hurt, but fortunately there was no loss of life.

Unfortunately for me, I was not there. Although I was still a member of the unit, I was in Ireland at the time and, given the antiquated telephone system that existed in Ireland in those days, I could not be contacted in sufficient time so I was excused. Today, I am sorry that I was not able to join my buddies for another event of historical significance.

SWIFT STRIKE THREE: FORT BRAGG, NORTH CAROLINA

Near the end of my tour of duty, the 20th Special Forces Group participated in a large scale "war game" at Ft Bragg, North Carolina. The purpose of this exercise was to test a new concept for delivering troops onto the battlefield. Vietnam was mostly jungle, not a lot of suitable drop zones for paratroopers. The 2nd Infantry Division—where I had trained troops—had been designated the 1st Calvary division, and helicopters were used so troops could rappel down fifty feet of rope, or land in tight places quickly. If you saw the movie *Apocalypse Now*, you are familiar with the concept.

Swift Strike Three included all of the Special Forces Groups, the two airborne divisions, the 82nd and the 101st, and these newly formed highly mobile forces. It was an enormous operation, and I only saw a small part, that being the 20th SF Group acting in their assigned role of jumping behind "enemy lines" and hooking up with "resistance fighters," just like we had been practicing before. Since I was a "short timer," I was initially assigned to staff, not going into the field by parachute but staying well behind the lines at headquarters. I no longer led an A-team in the 20th, so I was due for a promotion to a noncombat job. That news was a relief for me, because I had done the combat thing many times, and aside from the lack of creature comforts in the field, I always came back with a bad case of poison ivy that took weeks to cure.

At the last minute, like twenty-four hours from "D Day," someone up the chain of command decided that staff positions were not necessary, and that those so assigned would be assembled into additional A-teams going into the battle. I was assigned eleven men who I had never met, and most of them did not know each other. This, my friends, is no way to conduct special operations, even in training. A basic tenet of special operations units is the familiarity each member has with his teammates. Imagine a football team made up of total strangers—nobody knows how the other fellows will perform. It was a bad decision, but I did not have a vote. So, the next evening, my newest best friends and I boarded an old WWII C-47, loaded with supplies and equipment which had been quickly assembled, and lifted off for a three- to four-hour plane ride before reaching our destination. Our static lines had an extension of about fifteen feet, so we—and our chutes—would pass safely under the tail of the plane when we jumped. Our rucksacks were, as usual, con-nected to our parachute harness by quick releases and the drop line (about twenty-five feet) was stowed by rubber bands crisscrossing the top of our reserve chute.

We were actually relieved when the jump master signaled, "Ten minutes out." At last, we would be standing up after being seated uncomfortably for hours. At the "two minute signal," we stood up and started the normal routine: The commands are: GET READY–STAND UP–HOOK UP–CHECK EQUIPMENT–CHECK STATIC LINE—and ten seconds out, STAND IN THE DOOR. Now you watch the red and green light by the door. When it turns from red to green, we exit as quickly as possible. Remember, we are jumping from eight hundred feet, not a lot of time to correct any malfunction. And, at night, you want to know where your teammates are so assembling on the ground will be quick. I was first out the door, counted to four, looked up and saw a proper canopy—so far so good. Then, a malfunction.

At about one hundred feet above the drop zone, I released the quick releases on my rucksack, and it immediately fell toward the ground. But somehow during the long flight, the drop line had come loose from some of the rubber bands, and wrapped itself around my neck. I felt a burning sensation as the twenty-five-foot drop line took every ounce of skin off the back of my neck. And, because of the rucksack's weight, I was no longer in an upright position. So I would not be able to absorb the landing shock with my legs. Instead, I would land at about a forty-five-degree angle on my side. Fortunately, the only damage was to the back of my neck. The medic on the ground actually called his partner over to see the wound. He said, "That's the worst abrasion I have ever seen!"

I was extremely fortunate. If the drop line had interfered with my static line, I could have been dragged along behind the plane, no way to cut loose or be winched back into the plane. Newer aircraft used for airborne troops have a winch which can retrieve a helpless soul hanging out behind the plane. The school solution for this unfortunate situation was for the jumper to place both hands on top of his helmet. The jumpmaster, seeing this signal, would cut the static line, and the jumper would deploy his reserve parachute. As it was, I only had bruises from the landing, but the abrasion was a serious matter. We would be in the field for another week. How was I going to avoid an infection, much less deal with a painful wound that had to be screened from the summer sun in North Carolina? Captains do not question orders, and so I stayed in the woods with my "new team."

A week later, we were brought back to Ft. Bragg. The mission, in terms of proving that helicopters were the new airborne troopers' ride of the future, was a success. I had contracted my usual case of poison ivy, and the abrasion was beginning to heal. My attitude? I could not wait to be discharged and return to civilian life. Six years and fifty-plus jumps after joining the Green Berets, I had satisfied my obligation to the US Army.

Not too far in the future, the 1st Cav with their helicopters were dispatched to Vietnam, where they were cut up pretty badly in their first battles. The history of the Vietnam War is well known, and demonstrated the utter futility of sending large numbers of troops twelve thousand miles from home to fight an indigenous enemy. President Johnson and his advisors totally disregarded the well-recorded history of the defeat of foreign forces against a determined population. Sound familiar today?

SETTLING DOWN IN COLUMBUS

In the early 1960s, I lived in Columbus in a small apartment near the center of town. Life for me still centered on LeGrand and Lucy. Besides my military obligations, I began working in various business enterprises with LeGrand. It was small stuff, nothing on which to base a career on for a newly minted Yale graduate.

In 1960, my uncle, LeGrand's father, died after a long bout with prostate cancer. In that era, little was known about how to detect, or treat, a disease that affects most men at some time, if they live long enough. Most of my male relatives have had this problem. Genetics, I suppose. Fortunately for me, when I got that dreaded news at age sixty-five, modern medicine had proven treatments, and I selected surgery. After reviewing all the treatments available, I chose surgery—the so-called gold standard—and am still on this side of the grass as I approach my seventy-eighth birthday. Friends who went with radiation (or who simply denied they had a problem) are no longer with us in these earthly gardens.

At "Big's" funeral service, cousin Hunley presided. He had become an Episcopal minister, later to be elected a bishop for the diocese of East Carolina, the coastal region based in Wilmington, North Carolina. The service was at the Episcopal church in Columbus. As I recall, the then-presiding minister at that church was not particularly popular with the flock. Nothing worthy of defrocking, just dull and not capable of inspiring his members. I remember my father, Edgar, talking with Hunley after the service. "Hunley, if the congregation isn't happy with this leader, why can't they replace him?"

"Well, Eddie (as my father was known in the family circle), has he been taking money from the church coffers without permission?"

"Absolutely not!" my dad retorted.

"Well, is he having an affair· with someone in the congregation?"

My father, now back on his heels said, "NO!"

"Well, Eddie, if he is not guilty of some major offence, you are stuck with him. This thing is weighted pretty heavily in our favor!" As you can see, Hunley had a fine sense of humor.

Social life in Columbus was nice. We spent lots of time shooting, mostly doves and quail, riding horses in preparation for entering the fox hunting field, playing tennis or squash, and enjoying many fancy dinner parties. I had made friends with a few local fellows, now lawyers and businessmen, and I began to develop an uneasy feeling that the real world was passing me by. As a bachelor, my opportunities for female companionship were limited. There were a few local girls who were very attractive and unmarried but I had become used to a broader field up north where my friends and I would go to Bennett Junior College, Smith, and other girls' schools where there was a larger pool of possible mates. Back then, the girls' colleges were more famous for awarding more "Mrs. Degrees" than something leading to a career. Women were more or less expected to marry early and choose a husband who would be the bread winner while she would take care of the home front and the children.

After the somnolent decade that had gone before, the 1960s were a time of monumental change in the American way of life. My generation was on the leading edge of this change. Old rules were crumbling, the "pill" emancipated women—and men as well in terms of assuming responsibility for accidents. For all the bluster and chatter at Yale in the fifties, there was very little actual sexual activity. We were probably the least educated generation in matters of love, sex, and how to go about developing a good relationship with a prospective life partner.

But love was one thing. First I had to sort out my working life. I began to see very little possibility that LeGrand would, or could, lead a company to any particular heights, regardless of any help I could offer. He was obsessed with his wealthy friends in the northeast and in Texas, and seemed intent on chasing their lifestyle without the financial means to keep up.

My primary job was managing the bowling center we built in Columbus. I had never done something like this, so I was operating by the seat of my pants. When we opened, we were overwhelmed with customers.

Everybody in Columbus wanted to try bowling, a first of a kind experience in town. Initially, we were inundated with patrons, but just as quickly they went away. A fad for the social set, but not something on which we could base a business. My analysis was that bowling was a sport that would be attractive to the ordinary people, not the country club set. So, I thought about how to fill all twenty lanes with paying customers, morning and night. Mornings were the worst challenge, so I thought about housewives. Military families were living nearby, and their husbands were overseas, mostly in Vietnam. I put together a promotional plan for this group. I offered a six-week bowling clinic for women, weekday mornings between 10 a.m. and noon—bowling with a well-organized program. To promote this, I went door to door in selected neighborhoods, dressed in a business suit with name tag, inviting these military wives to join a bowling clinic, nominal charge of two dollars for bowling instruction, including free nursery and coffee and donuts. We quickly filled two mornings, and soon they were bringing their friends. I found that by knocking on one hundred doors, I would get ten students. The class was for six weeks, so when the classes ended I invited them to form a beginner's bowling league. The conversion rate was 90 percent. Bingo! I had filled the otherwise dead period, the morning hours, and they were telling their friends about this so starting more such classes was relatively easy. Before long, when their husbands returned from war, they were coming in on weekends to bowl with other couples, and that led to forming couples' leagues.

The next target was the companies in Columbus who employed large numbers of people- Royal Crown Cola, Tom's Peanuts, and some of the textile mills. Now we had company teams competing at night, Monday through Thursday. There were enough participants to run a double shift, one group starting at 6:30 p.m. followed by a group at 9:00 p.m. Basically, this effort kept the bowling center from going the way of many other centers that folded after the novelty was gone.

The next major problem I faced was the matter of how to maintain the Brunswick pinsetters, the automatic machines that replaced pin boys. These were mostly mechanical contraptions, with some electrical components. When we opened for business we hired a man from Tennessee who was a good bowler, and very adept at fixing problems that occasionally caused a machine to malfunction. Needless to say, we were totally dependent on him to keep us in business. As the resident expert, he developed an attitude, and became a serious problem. He would work when and if it suited him. When he announced that he was taking Thanksgiving off, and would be away for four days' vacation, I knew that I needed to do something. My solution was simple—I needed to learn how to do his job.

The Brunswick Company operated a school in Hershey, Pennsylvania to train pinsetter mechanics. It was a six-week course, so in February I drove to Hershey from Columbus to learn how to "disassemble and reassemble" the machine. The instruction was excellent, and I came back to Columbus confident that

I could do this fellow's job. Before firing him, I hired an assistant, an African American who worked in a service station nearby. J.D. Sampson could not sign his name, but he was a quick learner and handy with tools. It did not take me very long to show him enough so that he could handle the small stuff, and call me when he needed help. I fired the other guy, and we now had a pretty sweet operation going at the Bowlarama. On a few occasions, I would be called away from a black tie dinner party at LeGrand's home to come in through the back door, don my overalls and tackle a repair problem so the machine did not need to be shut down for the night. I bet not many Yale graduates know how to fix bowling machines.

In addition to school integration issues, businesses that served the public faced the same scrutiny. I had heard that Columbus business establishments were going to be the targeted. One day, about noon, I was in my office at the Bowlarama when four well-dressed African American men came in to see me. They asked me if they could bowl. I answered, "What size bowling shoes do you gentlemen need?"

They did not want to bowl, they wanted to know if they would be allowed to bowl. I told them that they would be welcome at anytime, but all the lanes were booked with league play from 6:00 p.m. through closing time. You can bowl now, or come back anytime we have lanes available, like early afternoon, or on the weekend when we had open bowling, no leagues. The situation was defused, and when they returned to bowl, I told my employees and regular customers that this was the law, and we were going to comply. We never had a problem integrating the Bowlarama.

J.D. Sampson became my most valuable employee. He learned to do virtually all the maintenance on all of our equipment and was totally reliable, never late or absent from work. We paid him much better than his old service station job, and, at his request, we were his "bank." We held some back from every paycheck, and gave it to him on request. I later learned that this helped him with his lady friends. When he died suddenly, I attended his funeral, but I was too emotional to speak when invited by his pastor.

A WATERSHED MOMENT

Two events, in my opinion, tipped the scale in LeGrand's life. First, his mother died after suffering a stroke. By that time, I was living in her home, taking on some of the duties of a nursing attendant. She had regular help during the day, but at night, I was there as the eyes and ears in case problems arose. The night she passed away, LeGrand and Lucy were in Ireland on one of their regular foxhunting trips. When the family doctor told me she was not going to recover, I managed to get a call through to LeGrand in Ireland to deliver the news. In those days, it took time to rearrange travel plans but when they eventually arrived home, I perceived a certain calm and peace in LeGrand. His mother had favored his brother, Shearen, and both parents had been hard on him, according to what my parents had told me. He was never really affirmed as a talented son and had, on several occasions, told me, "If I ever treat you like my parents have treated me, I hope you will speak up."

Now that his father and mother were gone, he was free to live as he wished. Happily for him, he had made some money in a restaurant deal that greatly enhanced his hip pocket appeal. His newfound freedom caused him to reexamine his marital relationship which, unfortunately, is not exactly an uncommon occurrence in our society. Women loved LeGrand. He was charming, attentive, a good dancer, and generally the life of the party. With no parental watchdogs, he was free to push the boundaries and stray. His wife, Lucy, was a nice lady but it was the old saying: "How you gonna keep 'em down on the farm after they've seen Paree?" Choate and Yale had opened his eyes to what the wider world had to offer and, on many occasions, he lamented his decision to leave New York City and the northeast behind. His parents had leaned on him to come home and now, as we have seen, I was replicating his error.

The opportunity to go into a major bank or international company had been there for the taking for me and my classmates. At recent reunions, most recently our fiftieth at Yale, I found I was not alone in having taken a wrong turn upon graduation. Several of my classmates expressed these same sentiments. They too had been pressured into returning home to carry on the family business. One friend told me that he had actually gone to work at Goldman Sachs but later had left to run the department stores his family owned in Arkansas. In my case, I did escape eventually but at great cost and with great risk.

It is useless to spend time speculating on things that might have been. Based on my record at Choate, Yale, and in the military, it is reasonable to assume that I would have been successful in corporate America.

When I consider my friends who went that route, I see many who rose to high positions and retired with wealth and families intact. But they did not have the worldly experiences that I enjoyed in LeGrand's world.

The second event that had an impact on LeGrand was my marriage to Kathleen Hudson. She was the most beautiful, accomplished woman I had ever met. Did I say woman? Well, that's stretching it a bit because she was still a senior in high school. To make it even more difficult, she lived in Atlanta. I was twenty-seven years old at the time, but I was not about to let the age difference put a stop to this romance, even though LeGrand did his best to block our path. He had been throwing me at the daughters of his wealthy friends in Texas and up north, but I knew none of them would agree to move to Columbus, especially as my compensation for working with LeGrand was well below their expectations. His best friend in Texas was John Blaffer, an heir to both the Humble Oil and Texaco fortunes. Blaffer once told me I should move to Houston, and he would introduce me to the young ladies as a wealthy land baron from Georgia. By the time they found out this was not true, it would be too late!

You are probably wondering how I met a high school girl in Atlanta. It has a lot to do with foxhunting in Ireland.

Prior to my introduction to Kathleen, I was in Ireland on at least four occasions, riding to the hounds with five different foxhound packs for most of the month of February. LeGrand, who was a regular, was good friends with Evan Williams, the Master of the

Tipperary Hounds. Evan was married to Gill, a British lady of high social standing, and they lived in County Limerick for the sport and also for tax reasons as many Brits were doing in that era. Evan and Gill had two sons, Hugh and Ian, both excellent horsemen and close to my age. In the hunt field, I joined up with the Williams boys and their friends who were very familiar with the countryside. Every hunt began by the Master meeting the local farmers in a nearby pub, and buying them a drink before we went off to gallop over their land. We Yanks, all two of us (me and LeGrand), were invited to this party, and the drink of choice was a large wineglass filled with port and brandy, in equal amounts. I considered it to be "liquid courage," because of the hazards of the sport. Then we would all mount up, and walk or trot to the starting point for the day's hunt.

The Master and his staff (called whips) would lead the pack of hounds into a cover, basically a thicket of perhaps one or two acres. The field (all the mounted spectators) were positioned at a distance, watching this performance. If the hounds pushed a fox out, the chase would be on. Our clue that action was eminent would be the hounds "speaking," that is, barking their peculiar sound, and leaving the cover in pursuit of their prey. Once the chase was on, the Master would blow "going away" on his horn, and that gave the field permission to follow along. At this point, I learned quickly to follow Hugh and Ian, as they knew which way the fox was most likely to go. As the field headed for the nearest gate behind the Master, we would wait a few moments to see if the hounds changed directions. More often than not, they did change course, and the field would be in a cue, passing through the gate in single file. Hugh and Ian would lead our little band on a shortcut, thus saving precious time. We wanted to see the hounds in pursuit, not just listen to them speaking as they followed the scent. The downside of this strategy was that it required us to jump several formidable obstacles in the blind. These obstacles consisted of a bank, about six to eight feet tall, with a water-filled ditch on either side. Often the bank was covered by thorn bushes, and you could not see what was on the other side. If we guessed correctly on the direction, and if we did not fall over or into the obstacle, we would be up front with the Master and the whips, with a front row seat to view the chase. In all my years riding with the hunt, I averaged falling—horse and rider—three times each season.

The sport in foxhunting is the chase, not killing the fox, which only happened a few times a season. Typically, the fox would run to ground, into a den, thus eluding the hounds. Needless to say, the Williams' boys and I became fast friends.

LeGrand and Lucy invited Hugh to visit us in Columbus, to see a bit of America, and to work part time with me in the bowling center. It was in July, and the heat and humidity were unbearable for someone accustomed to a high temperature of fifty degrees in Ireland that time of year. So, LeGrand told me to pick a cool place in the mountains of North Carolina, and take Hugh there for a week or so. I knew about a popular resort in Cashiers, North Carolina, frequented by southerners escaping the summer heat, so we went to the High Hampton Inn and Country Club. It was very rustic, but we did not care because the climate was delightful compared to Columbus.

Also in residence at High Hampton at the time was Kathleen Hudson, with her mother and younger brother, Paul. I noticed Kathleen on the tennis courts. She was stunningly beautiful, as well as an accomplished tennis player. I had no idea what her age might be, but she looked old enough for me to make an approach to her. Hugh and I hung out with the Hudsons, and so I got to know Kathleen as a friend. In the fall, I called her in Atlanta, asking if I could visit for the day. Her mother agreed, so a relationship started. I was a frequent visitor to Atlanta on day trips, driving back to Columbus after dinner. By springtime, we were an item. She applied to Wellesley and was accepted, so when summer arrived we were wondering how our relationship would withstand the forthcoming separation that would occur when she left for Wellesley in September. We continued to see each other through her freshman year at Wellesey. And then she took the plunge, left college and married me. LeGrand was still stuck with the wife of his parents' choosing when we married and he was, basically, jealous that I had acquired a young, beautiful bride. The conflict he created in our marriage led to the worst period of my life to date.

NEWLYWEDS

At first, LeGrand was interested in integrating Kathleen into our "Columbus lifestyle." She held her own brilliantly, especially considering her age. As a matter of fact, she was a big asset to the family. We became friends with some terrific couples of our own age, but there was always an underlying problem. The business prospects LeGrand was offering me did not match those of our friends.

Kathleen learned to shoot, and became quite proficient on the dove field, harvesting as many birds as her male counterparts. She became an excellent cook, and could put on a first-class dinner party with ease. One New Year's Eve, we invited twelve of our fiends to a black-tie dinner party at our home, and lit all the candles in the house, no electric lights at all. After dinner, we played dice, casino fashion, on the dining room table using a large box frame that I had built, with a felt cover on the table. I had visited the bank that afternoon and bought $500 in new one-dollar bills, which I exchanged with our guests to use for chips. The men knew how to play, and the ladies became very keen very quickly. It was a great party thoroughly enjoyed by all.

Since dove shooting was a regular activity for us, I had acquired a Labrador retriever to fetch the birds we shot. When that dog died, we decided to get not one but two replacements, one for me and one for Kathleen. We found a litter of puppies, black Labs with good pedigrees, and brought two of these youngsters into our home. They were very cute and hyperactive. One night, when we were hosting a dinner party for eight, the table was set and we were getting dressed when we heard a loud clatter coming from the dining room. We found both pups on top of the table, knocking Waterford crystal wineglasses about, and devouring two whole sticks of butter! Very soon thereafter, we were back down to only one retriever, and had a nice kennel in the backyard to prevent a recurrence.

I was running the bowling center we had built in Columbus, but LeGrand gradually lost interest in any ideas for expansion. He thought he had enough money to continue the overseas trips to Ireland and the north of England to foxhunt and shoot grouse, and soon he was invited to join the Okeetee Club in Ridgeland, South Carolina. At the time, there were only eighteen members and they owned 150,000 acres, all dedicated to shooting quail, ducks, and doves. The expense of operating the club was covered by the sale of timber. The land was typical South Carolina pine plantation, with a little hardwood and some low lying swamps, ideal terrain for upland game shooting. Through the auspices of his best friend, Samuel B. Webb, he became the first ever member of Okeetee who was not from the old Yankee aristocracy. LeGrand had met Sam in the army, where Sam had been his superior officer. Both were Yale graduates, a few years apart. Sam more or less adopted LeGrand and introduced him to the world of old-line wealth. Sam's mother was Electra Havemeyer Webb, his father J. Watson Webb (a Vanderbilt), and they lived in New York City and Shelbourne, Vermont. "Ma" Webb established a museum in Shelbourne, which is custodian to an impressive art collection as well as American artifacts that are unequalled in this country. On their honeymoon, Watson and Electra travelled to Europe where she befriended several impressionist painters and acquired a large number of their works. For his part, Watson was one of the top polo players of his era, a lefty who achieved a ten goal rating in the 1920s. Today, lefties are required to carry the mallet in their right hand to avoid traffic accidents on the field, a handicap that affected me when I played polo for about fifteen years in the eighties and nineties.

LeGrand idolized these families and bent over backward to amuse them. He was accepted warmly into their circles, but the problem for LeGrand was his absolute inability to keep up with them financially. The more he cultivated these friends, the less he focused on our little business operation. This began to weigh on me because I could see plainly that this was not good for my new family. Kathleen and I had two children, a son, LeGrand, born in 1967, and a daughter, Palmer, born in 1970. I became increasingly concerned as I contemplated our future. Meanwhile, LeGrand, still married to Lucy, was exercising his newfound freedom from parental scrutiny by seeking other women. At first, he felt guilty about his dalliances, but, conveniently, he eventually found a doctor who told him, "You should do what you feel like doing!" Talk about being given a free pass.

Obviously, his behavior was a concern to us, but it only got really tricky when he set his sights on the wife of one of our friends. She was young, rich, and fascinated by LeGrand's attention. Soon, LeGrand was asking Kathleen to help him facilitate secret rendezvous. She would pick up Betty at her home on the pretext of going off to play tennis and then deliver her to LeGrand. Obviously this was very awkward for us as it compromised our relationship with Betty and her husband. But how are you supposed to say no to your boss and benefactor? We felt trapped in this situation and feared financial consequences.

TIME FOR ACTION

To protect the innocent, I will cut to the bottom line. LeGrand's mental state began to deteriorate. He became more and more depressed about being trapped in an arranged marriage when all he wanted to do was break free and painlessly play the field. He divorced Lucy and eventually married Betty but she was not keen on supporting his sporting habits. The marriage was short-lived. He started to lose his mind and was briefly confined in a hospital where he received electric shock treatment. Inevitably, he became totally disengaged from our business. I realized that I had to get my family out of this trap. The tipping point came when LeGrand's brother, Shearen, who lived in Montgomery, called me to say, "Don't make business decisions without talking to me." I thought this was a bit rich because Shearen had never been involved in any of our business ventures and was not exactly a whiz at operating any kind of enterprise. He was a charming chap who had been a Wiffenpoof at Yale but was denied the opportunity to pursue a career in opera and theater by his parents who insisted he return to Montgomery to manage the family jewelry store. Same old story. Running a business was not Shearen's calling in life, and when it didn't work out, he became an entertainer, basing his act on Victor Borge, singing and playing the piano. He became a big hit, playing at conventions throughout the south and once even played for Ronald Reagan at the White House. However, the big time eluded him.

When I hung up from his call, I knew I had to do something. We had a few partners in the bowling centers after building another facility in Auburn, Alabama, and I called them, first to explain LeGrand's mental state and then to make them an offer—buy me out or let me buy their interest. They quickly took the latter option and decided to sell. So our problem was partially solved. Kathleen and I would be able to take total control of what we had, but the greater issue was how we should proceed in the future. I did not see any opportunity to go back north and search for the opportunities that would have been waiting for me when I graduated from Yale. Atlanta was a possibility, as it was Kathleen's home, but there seemed nothing interesting on the horizon there.

THE GREAT ESCAPE

I needed a new direction and it arrived through some friends in Columbus who were developing a residential resort community in Panama City on the northern gulf coast of Florida. They approached me about joining them in a marketing capacity. The money was good and the opportunity looked like a potential home run. So we accepted and moved to Bay Point, a beautiful property on St. Andrews Bay with golf, tennis, and a marina. We were selling condominiums and single-family home sites to folks from Memphis, Birmingham, Nashville, and Atlanta. The "gated club community" was a fairly new concept at the time so we were treading a little known path with only the Sea Pines Plantation on Hilton Head Island, South Carolina, as a beacon for what could be successfully achieved. We were not alone in trying to capitalize on the concept.

Panama City, Florida, was Wild West country in the early 1970s. There were honky-tonk joints up and down the beach which were frequented by the executives from all the resorts being developed in the area. Also the ancillary personnel involved—lawyers, architects, and building contractors—were hanging out there as often as possible, chatting up the girls who were numerous and readily available. For me, it was like going from the frying pan into the fire. I had escaped from the problem in Columbus, Georgia, only to land in a place where there was an entirely different kind of problem, mainly being unfaithful to one's spouse. We were continually entertaining real estate clients and club members, using our fleet of boats to take them fishing, snorkeling, and for trips to parts of the beach not accessible by car. Back in Georgia, we had at least been surrounded by stable married couples who were doing the normal sort of family things, working at typical jobs, and carrying on a normal social life. Here we were always in party mood which caused major problems for a lot of us, including yours truly. You have heard the old saying, "Everybody is doing it." A poor rationalization for extramarital activity, but often cited as an excuse.

One of our favorite activities was taking our boats—a collection of twenty-two- to twenty-six-foot open-configuration center-console vessels—out to Hurricane Island, daytime and at night. This island was created when the channel from St. Andrews Bay into the Gulf of Mexico was opened. It cut off a part of the coastline from the mainland. A local developer had built a "party palace" on the island—thatched roof, open air, no power, only generator and candles, but very seductive, romantic, and isolated. The structure was built on pilings, well above the high watermark, looking out over the Gulf to the south and St. Andrews Bay to the north. There was something wrong with you if you did not love this place.

We locals and our guests were regular visitors. Parties ranged from hard "R" to soft "X." Like, "What were the Romans doing at the last moment?" An old southern joke's punch line is, after the church service at the picnic, more souls were begot than saved!

On a more civilized note, one of our friends was Charles Ireland, then Chairman of Vulcan Materials in Birmingham. Charles and his wife Caroline became good pals. They lived part time on a major estate near Bay Point, on the bay. Charles and I shared the same birth date, November 29, and the two couples always celebrated together, usually at their compound, with near-frozen vodka and caviar. Charles had been around Panama City for years, and had some interesting friends of considerable means. We decided to start a wine tasting society, twelve members as I recollect, and we met once a month when one of us would host a formal dinner with special wines. We were, for the most part, buying wine futures from a merchant in Atlanta, taking delivery twelve months later. At the time, we were buying 1961 Bordeauxs and 1966 Burgundys for about $20 per bottle. Lafite Rothschild, Romanee Conte, Le Tache—only the best. After a year of this excess, we decided to close down, and have a big party at Bay Point to celebrate the event. The plan was to have dinner for the wine group, and then have all our friends come for a dance party. I suggested getting Peter Duchin's orchestra to play for the dancing. I had known Peter at Yale, and now he had a prominent society band.

The date was set, Duchin on board, and all apparently in order. However, the weather intervened. A major storm hit the west coast of Florida, rendering all modes of air transit impossible. Duchin and I spoke several times about solutions, but prospects were dim that we could have a band for our party. I told Peter, "Just do what you can to get enough musicians here to make some music." Well, he pulled a rabbit out of the hat, and actually got the full complement of players on site, only about an hour late. He rushed in, and said they would set up and begin playing ASAP. Having been in this position with my Yale Bullpups, I told him, "No, feed your guys and give them some liquid libation, then when you are ready, start the gig."

The evening was a total success, thoroughly enjoyed by one and all. Years later, in Newport, Peter was playing for the Preservation Ball at the Elms. When Jane and I walked in, he stopped me, and introduced me to his musicians for the evening. He told them, "This is the fellow who gave us food and drink after a hellish journey to Panama City, Florida, before having us start playing."

REALITY BITES

There were many good times at Bay Point. However, it was a fairyland, not destined to continue. I learned very quickly that the partners in this venture had no experience in building and financing such a complicated project which involved millions of dollars. In the beginning, there were many banks and lending institutions throwing money at us, offering to take out the previous lender and basically provide us with 110 percent financing if we wished because everyone thought there was no limit to how high the property values would eventually go. Sadly, that merry-go-round always stops at some point and you have to face a day of reckoning. If you are not generating enough cash flow through real estate sales to pay the interest on the debt, you are obviously in serious trouble. In this instance, the catalyst for the day of reckoning came out of the Middle East when the Saudis and other Arab countries confiscated the oil fields and immediately raised the price of oil from three dollars a barrel to eleven dollars a barrel. It was 1973 and the prices we paid for virtually everything were never the same again. The bankers who had been calling to throw more money at us were now on the phone wanting to know how we intended to repay the loan. Bay Point was officially bankrupt.

I no longer had a salary from Bay Point, but, fortunately, I had obtained a Florida real estate license and I still owned the two bowling centers back in Columbus, Georgia, and Auburn, Alabama. So I opened a general real estate office in Panama City with a partner and began to work on various commercial real estate ventures. I also set about trying to sell the two bowling centers. Cousin LeGrand, now partially recovered and married again, to his third and final wife, was eager to own the bowling center in Columbus and a chain operator from Mobile, Alabama, bought the Auburn center. I did not want to go back to Columbus or Auburn and run bowling centers. I wanted, like the proverbial mouse, no cheese just to get my head out of this trap.

Salvation came, as it has many times in my life, when my friend Scott Morrison, who had been at Bay Point briefly as head of resort operations, joined a relatively new venture in South Carolina at Kiawah Island which was being developed by the Kuwait Investment Company. The money was coming from the Middle East. By expropriating the oil fields, the Arabs had become major players on the world scene overnight and one of their first ventures was the island known as Kiawah near Charleston. They contracted with Charles Frasier, of Sea Pines' fame, to manage the development and he installed some of his best executives to move the project forward. But even the Arabs did not like paying exorbitant fees and soon fell out with Frasier who was dismissed. However, many of his executives were hired to stay on and run the development. Enter Scott Morrison, one of the most talented resort mangers I have ever known. He was responsible for all food, beverage, golf, tennis, condominium management, and other resort operations. Scott and I had become friends at Bay Point, and when he arrived at Kiawah, he suggested I follow him and join his new venture. Fortunately, on Scott's recommendation, I was added to the real estate sales team. My other possible escape route had been to join the Johns Island development at Vero Beach, Florida, but Kathleen was lobbying for the Charleston area as it was close to her home in Atlanta and she had a few friends there. Happily, once I saw Kiawah and met the management team, I was sold.

They were by far the most talented people in the resort development business at the time. Pat McKinney, head of the sales operation, was the absolute best in the business I have ever encountered, before or after Kiawah. Pat came from a family of modest circumstances just like I did, worked his way through school, sold bibles door to door, and eventually joined the Sea Pines Group with Charles Frasier as a real estate salesman. Although he is my junior by a decade or more, I can say with complete confidence that I learned more from him than anyone I ever worked with anywhere. We are still friends today and we enjoy seeing him and his lovely wife Pam in Charleston several times a year as we travel north for the summer to Newport, Rhode Island.

For me, moving to Charleston meant moving back to a stable, family-oriented scene like the one I had enjoyed briefly in Columbus. After all the drama of LeGrand's life and the wild west, loose living scene in Panama City, I thought we were in a place where we could once again live a normal life, raise our children, and have a rewarding career in a wonderful environment. We immediately made many friends, and our connection with Kiawah was a major benefit.

I had made so many mistakes, bad mistakes which I would be embarrassed to enumerate, had hurt my family and my relationship with Kathleen, and now I felt all that was in the rearview mirror. We were making a fresh start and I was optimistic that all our problems were behind us.

BOMBSHELL

As the saying goes, there is nothing as permanent as change, and it suddenly became all too permanent and drastic for me. Among the many friends we made in Charleston was a young and wealthy bachelor who became an almost constant part of our life and social activity. He even went to New York with us, on our regular trip to the US Tennis Championships at Forest Hills. We hung out with Gene Scott, Vitas Gerulaitis, Ilie Nastase, and other top players of the day. Billy Talbert was the tournament director, and he treated us royally—best seats for all matches, access to the players (there was not much security for the players back then, not at all like it is today at Flushing Meadows). Perhaps I should have seen it coming. But it was not long before a romance blossomed, and Kathleen decided to leave me and marry him. After all I had put her through, I could understand her pursuit of a new and perhaps more stable life. All my bad decisions and behavior came home to roost and I had nobody to blame but myself. When I realized that this was her choice and her mind was made up, I did not resist. It was my destiny to be punished, lose my wife and children, and go out into the world to start over. This was the beginning of a journey for me, heading into unknown territory, basically starting over and scrapping the life I had lived after Yale. What a mess I had made of things after Yale—why had I gone to work for LeGrand in the first place? I should have been smart enough to see through the smoke and mirrors of LeGrand's world. I had enjoyed much sporting activity and met many interesting people, but it was not a realistic life. Fleeing to Bay Point turned out to be a bad decision and now the immediate future was looking very uncertain.

Nothing was made any easier by the fact that a management shakeup was brewing at Kiawah. The Kuwaitis, who owned the place, were dealing harshly with their senior managers, which was a foolish thing to do as these were the folks who made the company one of the most successful residential resort developments in the world. But the Arabs were new to the game and had no idea what made a real estate development work so that it could become financially successful. I distinctly remember a conversation with a young Kuwaiti company executive who had been sent to watch over us. Saleh al Zumin had an MBA in finance from Ohio State University and thought he was an expert in our business. He was driving with me down to Hilton Head Island to look at a new real estate product being built, a product we wanted to consider for Kiawah.

On the trip, I asked him how old he was, just a casual question, no offence intended.

"About twenty-eight," he replied.

Strange answer, I thought. So I tried again. "Twenty-eight or about to be twenty-eight?"

Finally, he said, "I don't know my age. I was born in a mud hut with no electricity and no birth records were kept for me and my sixteen brothers and sisters."

It was difficult for us, living in the good old USA, to understand the mindset of these people who, until they took over the oil fields, lived in a world that might have existed several hundred years ago. Now they were our overseers, questioning marketing and management decisions. We knew from our experience that we were selling the "sizzle," not the steak. We also knew how to manage the finances so as not to go the route of Bay Point. They were clueless.

LIFE GOES ON

Now, I needed to adjust to life without Kathleen. I moved into Fort Sumter House, a historic condominium right on the battery in downtown Charleston. It was a convenient location, and my children could walk down the street to visit me. I commuted to Kiawah every day, about a thirty-minute drive, and returned in the evening to go out on the town with some new friends. John Fort, Bill Douglas, and John Sutcliff were my constant companions. They were playing "cow pasture polo" on a farm just across the James River, and occasionally going up to Camden on the weekends, where games were being played by some more seasoned, accomplished players. Heath Manning and his sons would come from Columbia, and for the first time, I saw how the game should be played. Bill Douglas prevailed on the guys to let me borrow a horse and try my hand in a real game. It was a bit frightening because I did not have a good grasp of the rules, it was fast action, and I was always getting in somebody's way. However, I was hooked, and soon owned three horses.

Meanwhile, back at Kiawah, there was trouble brewing in the kingdom. When I had arrived on the scene, Frank Brumley was the General Manager, Lovick Sudduth was director of all matters to do with real estate, Scott Morrison was director of resort operations, and Pat McKinney was head of the real estate sales staff. This was an all-star lineup, like the NFL Pro Bowl. Superb managers all, and dearly loved by all employees. In July of 1978, Frank suddenly departed. I had heard that he was having difficulties convincing the Kuwaitis to create a pension or profit sharing plan for the employees, and perhaps this led him to resign, or he was fired. Lovick was immediately elevated to the position of Interim General Manager. Everybody loved Lovick, so life went on for the time being.

The fiscal year ended October 31, and department heads and sales staff were invited to a celebration in the executive offices. We had just completed a banner year, both in real estate sold and in resort occupancy. Everyone was in good spirits. During the party, Sal, the Kuwaiti watchdog, took Lovick outside to introduce him to his replacement, Gus Gilfillan. We were shocked! The company had been running like a Swiss watch under Lovick, and here was this new guy who none of us had met or knew anything about, becoming our leader.

In short order, Lovick resigned, and then Pat left shortly thereafter. Gus turned out to be not only incompetent but arrogant. Without Pat, there was no leader in the sales office. Gus called a meeting of the salesmen and asked if anyone would like to apply for Pat's job. I was the only one to raise my hand. I viewed it as a stepping stone, a chance to gain a title and get some good management experience. The other fellows were much better established with solid client bases, and their personal lives were more or less sound. They did not want any part of dealing daily with Gus. They were perfectly happy to keep on selling property, making good money, and confident that they had job security because of their existing client bases. For me, life in Charleston was not completely comfortable, because my former wife and her soon-to-be new husband were prominent in local society. I had been thinking about moving on, but felt the experience of being responsible for the Kiawah sales operation would be a feather in my cap when interviewing elsewhere.

I got the job, and basically carried on Pat's program with very little change. I did convince Gus and Sal to try a new strategy for the initial offering of home sites around the new Jack Nicklaus–designed golf course still under construction. Real estate was hot and demand for Kiawah product was very strong. So, I suggested we offer only twelve lots in the first release, and set much higher prices than had ever been achieved. My theory was that, if they did not sell because of price resistance, we could come out with another release at lower prices. Why not try it? We had nothing to lose as there were several hundred golf course lots being developed. Well, it did work. It was highly profitable for the company, and it established a new plateau for future sales.

Gus had an annoying habit of calling staff meetings for 5:00 p.m., and keeping them going until ten or eleven at night. A total waste of time, as nothing was ever decided that late. Lovick's meetings lasted about thirty minutes and much was accomplished. Soon, Scott Morrison left to join The Boca Raton Hotel and Resort. I was thinking about departing, but had not yet found a place to land.

In April, Bill Douglas suggested we drive down to West Palm Beach, where a new polo club was under development way out west, in what is now Wellington. They were advertising a big time polo match between the best American players and a team from Argentina. They called the event "The World Cup." So, Bill and I took off in my Jaguar sedan headed for this new polo Mecca. When we arrived, I immediately recognized another gated community in its early stages of development. They had about four or five polo fields, and a small group of townhome-type condos. Some distance away, they also had a golf and tennis complex with a clubhouse. The money was coming from a Fortune 500 company, Gould Inc., based in Chicago. The Chairman and CEO was Bill Ylvisaker, who wanted to remake the company into a widely diversified conglomerate. He also happened to be a very good polo player, and he wanted to create an exclusive club, an "Everglades Club West," featuring polo along with golf, tennis, etc. I met some of his management team members, and learned they were actively looking for a sales/marketing person with experience in high-end, exclusive-type properties. Yes, I said, I would be interested in interviewing for that position!

I was invited to come to headquarters in Chicago, to meet Ylvisaker himself. He intended to make this selection personally, as his on-site team was more suited to a Wellington-type community (think Levitt Homes on Long Island) than a first-class private club.

Bill and I hit it off perfectly. He also was a Yalie (a few years before my time), a member of Book & Snake, my senior society, and good at tennis as well as polo. It could not have been a better fit. He knew all about Kiawah, and was mightily impressed at what was happening there. Fortunately, he did not know about Gus, only the original team!

LAST DAYS IN CHARLESTON

Prior to my trip with Bill Douglas to see the World Cup polo match, I was adjusting to my new life as a single man in Charleston. I was in my thirties, good tennis player, aspiring polo player, and in good shape financially, besides being a well-read Yale graduate with social skills. Although there were not a lot of attractive young women available in Charleston at the time, I managed to find a steady flow of willing partners with whom I could enjoy female companionship. This was the seventies and social mores had changed. Women's lib, the pill. It was not Panama City by any means, but it was a moderately swinging time in Charleston. Disco was popular and the Bee Gees with their falsetto voices were all the rage.

Before Kathleen could become Mrs. John Rivers, she needed a legal divorce from me. The South Carolina laws on divorce were, at that time, draconian. There was a mandatory two-year waiting period, and a filing of a "suit for cause." One of us would need to file a claim of adultery. There was no such thing as a no-fault divorce. Neither of us wanted to go through that process. Kathleen presented me with a plan: She had discovered that one could obtain a legal divorce in Haiti, provided both parties were agreeable. So, she made the trip and returned in a few days with an official looking document, written in French, bearing a court stamp and adorned with red ribbons. Apparently, South Carolina would accept a divorce granted in another jurisdiction, once again if both parties were in agreement.

My greatest concern about leaving Charleston was putting seven hundred miles between me and my children. LeGrand and Palmer were of tender age, and would henceforth be under the roof of a stepfather with their mother. Kathleen was very cooperative regarding visitation, and I felt John had their best interests at heart. Still, it was a bitter pill for me to swallow. Through the years to come, I publicly thanked John for all he did for my children, including toasting him to this effect at both kids' weddings much later. We did not always agree, particularly when it came time to select prep schools and colleges, but from my observation of other fractured families, we did better than most.

When I handed my resignation to Gus, he tried to persuade me to reconsider. Failing there, he asked my advice regarding my replacement, perhaps someone on the sales staff. I immediately named Hal Ravenel as the perfect choice. When Gus asked why I thought Hal was the best choice, I answered, "He has been here a long time, knows the property well, and is a native

Charlestonian. So, Hal is less likely to leave you than the rest of us!"

In the fall of 1979, I put Charleston in my rearview window and struck out for Palm Beach.

ARRIVAL AT PALM BEACH POLO & COUNTRY CLUB

Exactly twenty years after graduating from Yale, I was going to my third residential resort property. At Bay Point, I had learned all the things *not* to do to be successful in this business, and at Kiawah, I learned all the things *to* do to be successful. Now, I was going to be part of shaping a new project, with the financial backing of a Fortune 500 company but staffed by people with little, if any, experience in the high-end market. There was no organizational chart with clear lines of reporting. Palm Beach Polo & Country Club was made up of approximately 2,500 acres, carved out of the greater Wellington community. When I arrived, it included a golf and tennis club, with a few condos which had been built to serve Wellington but was now part of this new, private club. About three miles away, the polo complex was under construction. Several polo fields, a stadium, and a few condos were competing and a clubhouse was under construction. The land in between these two ends of the property was undeveloped. To travel from one to the other, one had to use the public roads.

The Wellington staff and the PBPCC staff were somewhat interconnected. Since PBPCC was the new kid on the block, the Wellington staff tended to try to manage the PBPCC staff. Also, PBPCC was sexy, Wellington was plain vanilla, so everybody wanted to get in on the act. The manager of the polo part was Jim Plymire, an older man who had been involved with several small club developments on the ocean, just south of Palm Beach. He also had been involved with a mountain club in North Carolina. However, he had no experience with the type of project Ylvisaker envisioned. Bill's daughter, Laurie Ylvisaker, was head of marketing. Allan and Maggy Scherer were a husband/wife team, brought in from California because they were well connected to the polo community to whom we intended to sell property. I was supposed to take over the sales operation, but I immediately realized that others wanted to micromanage me. The Wellington marketing team was very good at handling a lower middle class subdivision, but their strategies were not compatible with a PBPCC-type project. Nonetheless, they were trying to impose their program on me.

Fortunately, Bill Ylvisaker was the big boss, and he understood the need to separate the marketing functions of the two projects. Still, there was always some underlying conflict.

When I asked Jim Plymire to show me the development plan for the land connecting the two ends of PBPCC, he pulled a couple of large sheets of paper out of his desk, showing his personal drawing of a concept, basically a maze of cul-de-sacs scattered all over the place. This was my first opportunity to show my worth, by explaining how Kiawah had a "spine road" to move traffic easily from one end of the island to the other end. Small subdivisions were accessed by "exit roads," thereby preserving the small exclusive community feeling while still providing easy access throughout the property. The Interstate Highway System functions that way between cities all over the US.

He agreed to hire our Kiawah land planner, Rob Hull, who had developed this concept, to come down as a consultant and lay out our spine road. Rob was paid $3,000 for his work, and without his input, no telling what kind of congestion and aggravation PBPCC would have experienced. Rob was fighting a battle with cancer, and died shortly thereafter. He did not live to see how critical his plan had been to the success of PBPCC.

PBPCC was a very social operation, with regular parties entertaining people from Palm Beach and prospects flying down from New York on the Gould corporate jet. Polo enthusiasts from around the world began to show up, and many bought property. Players from the major polo hubs in the US were our strongest market initially. Norman Brinker from Dallas; Seth Herndon and Dick Albert from Oklahoma; Steve Goss from San Antonio; the Armstrong family from Texas; the Orthwein/Busch families from St. Louis; Peter Brant from Greenwich, Connecticut; Skee Johnston from Chattanooga. They all wanted to see, and be a part of, the new polo Mecca for the winter months. Part of the PBPCC's success must be attributed to Royal Palm Polo Club in Boca Raton. John Oxley, an oil man from Oklahoma, had built his club a few years earlier. It was strictly a polo club, no golf, tennis, or social pretensions. His club was a Ford compared to Ylvisaker's Rolls Royce. The irony here is that John Oxley was a large shareholder in Gould, and here was Gould's chairman using company money to build his "personal" club, with many extra features. Royal Palm Polo had brought a fair number of polo players to the neighborhood. PBPCC was essentially a better "mouse trap," so we had a built-in clientele just thirty miles to the south. Oxley was none too pleased, but he wanted to play in tournaments at PBPCC, as did most of his members.

Personally, my polo skills were improving, under the guidance of Allan Scherer and his sons, Brad and Warren, all of whom were highly ranked payers. Plus, there was the annual migration of Argentine players, both professionals and grooms, who were worth studying. The polo fields were like golf greens and fairways. How could you miss hitting a ball under such ideal circumstances? I quickly realized that my horses were nowhere near good enough for this level, so I began retooling. Since I was a good prospect to buy horses, all the pros who were selling horses were my newest best friends, and also coaches.

Real estate sales were moving along nicely, but the management situation was not improving. The Wellington staffers really wanted to play a role in this exciting venture. Some of them actually began playing polo themselves.

The first sign of trouble occurred when the CFO from Gould asked me to prepare a sales plan for the next year. Based on all the data, I projected condominium sales at sixty units, at the then prevailing prices. The CFO looked at me as if I had lost my mind. He needed a budget of 150 sales to make the numbers work. I knew that was not possible, and if I submitted that plan, I would probably be blamed for the shortfall and fired. After a rather heated discussion, I suggested he write a financial plan based on my realistic projection of sixty sales.

By now, I was pretty well established in the community, making sales and giving good advice when asked. Suddenly, I had a brilliant idea: what if I could give up the management position but remain as a real estate salesman, working on commission, for company property (plus land outside the club)? I was still "on the team," promoting PBPCC and visiting the UK for the summer polo season (with expenses paid by the club), plus being a resident advisor. If I was not receiving a paycheck from Gould, how could they fire me if sales did not meet their expectations? Besides, this would calm the troubled waters between the Wellington and PBPCC staffs, as I was the focal point of most disputes. I presented the plan, and they accepted. Being an independent contractor, receiving some expense reimbursement, was far better for me, and more convenient for them.

Over the next five years, I sold millions of dollars' worth of property in and around PBPCC, and made more money than I ever imagined possible.

As more people arrived at PBPCC, the social activity increased exponentially. The main weekly event was Sunday polo with the featured match in the stadium, preceded by a fancy luncheon and followed by a drinks party that went on into the night. Usually I would play in a practice game in the morning, then join the luncheon event. Many Palm Beachers attended this event, as did every good looking single woman within thirty miles. It was like a singles bar in New York, everybody on the prowl. If you were a polo player, you were virtually guaranteed success. There was social activity almost every night at the many restaurants and bars nearby, and often an invitation to some soiree in Palm Beach. Helen Boehm (of Boehm Porcelain fame) sponsored a major black tie party at the newly opened Polo Clubhouse with the Peter Duchin orchestra and the Yale Wiffenpoofs on a Friday evening. We were entertaining a large number of visitors (guests of Ylvisaker) who had come down for the weekend, as usual, on the Gould jet as well as commercial airlines. It was at this party that I met Pamela Parry, who would become the next Mrs. Elebash.

POLO IN ENGLAND
AND GERMANY

Before continuing into the saga of my marriage to Pam, I want to talk about one of my most memorable experiences in polo. Many players were coming to PBPCC from Europe. The high season for polo in the UK was June, July, and August, and Guards Polo near Windsor Castle, just a short drive from London, was the most popular venue. I had met and befriended some of these folks, and I was charged with visiting there to promote PBPCC. Some of the players lent me horses, so I could play in practice games at Guards and at Cowdray Park located near Midhurst in Sussex. For two years, I was enjoying this experience, meeting many new friends, and developing prospects for PBPCC.

I had visited London many times in the 1960s, going to and from Ireland for foxhunting and for skiing in Switzerland. The routine was to fly first to London for a few days, then on to the other venue. On my first visit, I was struck by the class system that was in place. This was more than rich versus poor. It prevailed in all levels of society. The hall porter aspired only to be the best hall porter, not to break out to a more important position.

In the USA, everybody wants to move up the totem pole, and it is entirely possible to do so. Nothing about London resembled the USA—cars, traffic signs, taxis, buses—and the left side driving took all my concentration to avoid collisions, especially at the roundabouts. The restaurant menus did not have familiar offerings, and the way meals were prepared was different. It took several visits before I was comfortable moving about the city and ordering in restaurants.

By my second visit, I was shopping in St. James and on Saville Row. Custom-made suits and shirts were cheaper in London than in New York at the time. My first pair of bespoke shoes made at Maxwell's cost about $60. These were the style of clothes cousin LeGrand was wearing, and I copied him. I remember when the pound was valued at $1.01. I also remember the pound being worth four times a dollar. Over those years, I was completely dressed by London merchants. The last item I bought was a tuxedo, at Huntsman. It was a beautifully made garment—two pair of trousers with that "slant back" feature so it covered one's heel without breaking in the front, the coat sleeves were cuffed, with buttons, and a vest was included. The price was $600. Today the same outfit would cost several thousand dollars.

Our trip usually started in Atlanta, flying to JFK in New York. The British Air flight left from JFK departing early evening, arriving at Heathrow about 7:00 a.m. the next morning. By the time we cleared customs, collected baggage, and took a taxi into London, it would be 11:00 a.m., too early to check into our rooms, so we would drop the luggage with the hall porter and take a taxi to Wilton's, a terrific seafood restaurant in St. James. All of the wait staff were "old dears," ladies over the age of sixty, dressed in black maids' dresses with white aprons. My favorite lunch was Dublin Bay prawns to start, followed by Dover sole accompanied by a nice white burgundy. Then came the stilton cheese with several glasses of vintage port. By the time we finished, we could barely keep our eyes open, so we went back to our hotel for a long nap. The evening began with a cocktail in the hotel's bar, and then we were off to the theater, or a concert. Dinner was after the theater and it was back to the hotel to rest up for the next day's activities.

On one of these trips, we were able to get tickets to see Margot Fonteyn and Rudolp Nureyev dance at Covent Garden. The performance was sold out, but I took a chance and visited the ticket office late afternoon. As I approached the box office, a gentleman suddenly appeared, wanting to give up his tickets for the night's performance. That was an incredible stroke of luck for us.

We also heard the Band of the Coldstream Guards at Royal Albert Hall playing the 1812 Overture, visited all the major museums, and saw all the usual attractions, like the Tower of London.

So, I was no stranger to London as I went to play polo and promote PBPCC. London had changed since my last visit. Investment banks were opening offices and other industries were flourishing as well. There was definitely a more cosmopolitan feel to the city.

My best friend was Sir Raymond Brown and his family. They lived just a short distance from Guards, and they invited me frequently to their parties. All the top players, like Julian and Howard Hipwood, attended, and sometimes Prince Charles would be there. This was prior to his marriage to Diana. He was always warm and friendly to strangers like me.

Ray Brown had been knighted by the Queen for his wartime service. Early on, he founded Racal Electronics, a smaller version of IBM. His son, Martin, was a five-goal player, and we had met in a practice game at Royal Palm Polo Club in Boca Raton the previous season. Later, Ray would become godfather to my youngest son, Billy.

What a way to spend the summer months, living in a hotel in London, hanging out with the polo crowd, and enjoying the nightlife with my new friends. One of my first experiences at Guards involved taking a shower after a game before heading over to the Brown's for a BBQ. It was a chilly 58-degree late afternoon that day, and the showers had no hot water. Bracing, to say the least! This problem was corrected the following season. I particularly liked the theater, and saw many first-rate plays which never made it to the US. Two that stand out: The life story of Elvis Presley titled *Are You Lonesome Tonight*. Two different actors played the young Elvis and the old paranoid one just before he died. When the young Elvis was on stage, playing rock 'n' roll with his band, patrons in the theater were literally climbing up on the stage to dance. The other play was a drama, starring Anthony Quayle as the only actor. This was *Breaking the Code*, a thriller about the German enigma code in WWII.

Another new friend from the European polo contingent was Peter Schuster, a German who lived in Hamburg. He invited me to come for a visit during the German Polo Championships in August, and I quickly accepted. Peter had grown up during the reconstruction of Germany following WWII. Life was hard for youngsters in that situation, and he was determined to become a financial success. He became an architect and builder, developing a solid business in Germany. When the Arabs took over the oil fields, he told his wife, Ulla, "I must go to Saudi Arabia. They have all the money now and I must work for them." He had no contacts in the Arab world, but he was not shy about making blind calls. Eventually he made connections with the royal family, and was commissioned to design and build palaces and commercial buildings for them. He became a wealthy man, and was thoroughly enjoying playing polo in Germany and at PBPCC. He never played in the UK, as his German season ran at the same time.

Peter entertained me, and my then wife, Pam, royally. Compared to the US, prices of everything in Germany then were astronomical. Dinner for four at the Harborside restaurant ran about $1,000. We stayed with Ulla and Peter in their home (more like a castle) for a week. As the German Championships were about to begin, Peter took me aside and asked, "Would you agree to be one of the mounted officials for the game? We want you, and a British officer with the Army of the Rhine to be our umpires."

"Why don't you use your club players?" I asked.

"We don't trust them. All of our players want you and the Brit, because we think you are honest." We agreed, even though neither of us was a fully trained umpire.

We all went to a fieldside picnic the day of the big game, the final match that would crown the German champion. I was shocked to see most of the players drinking vodka or wine. Never would that happen in the US. The sport is dangerous enough as it is, even if you are sober!

Just before the game started, my fellow umpire, a British army major, said to me, "See here, Mr. Elebash, I say we only call the most flagrant fouls. These people use their horses as battering rams. Let the Huns have at it!" As play began, I thought the Major had underestimated the situation. It was *the* roughest, most dangerous polo match I had ever witnessed. Fortunately, there were no serious injuries, and all players said we had been fair.

A few years later, Peter was badly injured playing in Berlin. I heard the news while I was playing in Saratoga. The prognosis was, at best, paralyzed from the neck down. Amazingly, he recovered after multiple surgeries, and began playing again at PBPCC. Soon he fell again, on his head, and never recovered. He died within days.

LIFE WITH PAM

Pam lived in Palm Beach. She had a business degree from Babson College, and was working with her mother managing what she referred to as "the family companies." She was a member of both the B&T and the Everglades Club. She was very close with Bill and Lynn Cudahy, a prominent couple in Palm Beach, who were very active in governance at both clubs. Bill, along with Byron Ramsing and Horton Prudden, were the leaders on both club boards. Bill's son (by a previous marriage) was a classmate of mine at Yale. Sadly, he committed suicide within a few years of graduation.

Pam was soft spoken, reserved, and quite good looking. She had the most interesting eyes of anyone I had ever seen. We start dating, and things were going well. I met her mother, Grace (AKA Gere) Parry, who had been a widow for many years. Initially, Gere did not pay much attention to us, was always reasonably pleasant, and we did not see much of her. She lived on the ocean in a spacious condominium in Boca Raton. Pam was always a bit mysterious about the family business, but that was of no concern to me at the time. I was

growing weary of new girls every week after polo, and
began to think this might be a reasonable choice for my
next wife. I was on the rebound from Kathleen. On the
surface, everything looked good, no flashing red lights.
So, we eventually talked about marriage. At one point,
I developed a bad case of cold feet, and attempted to
cut off the relationship. The very next day, she appeared
at my front door in PBPCC, and calmly talked about
how nice it would be to stay together, no pressure or
sense of urgency, totally calm, cool, and collected. Well,
my misgivings vanished and we proceeded to the altar.
We were married in a private ceremony in a garden at
the Everglades Club, with the Episcopal minister from
Bethesda officiating.

We decided to live in her beachfront condo in Palm
Beach, and I would commute to PBPCC for work. Pam
had been in this condo, owned by one of the companies, for a number of years rent free. Shortly after we
married, Gere began demanding we pay rent to the
company. She was also intruding into our lives in other
ways. I think she was jealous of her daughter who now
had a husband, and she did not. At some point, I asked
Pam to explain the companies to me—who owns control, and what do they do? For the first time, I learned
about the existence of her aunt, her late father's sister, who lived in Miami. The companies owned residential rental properties in the worst neighborhoods of
Miami. Aunt Margaret owned just under 50 percent of
the shares, Pam's mother owned about 30 percent, and
Pam owned the rest. Gere had been using them as her
personal piggy bank, and there was a crooked account-

ant overseeing Aunt Margaret's other assets, which were considerable.

Eventually, the pressure from Gere caused us to look for a way out of this trap. I suggested to Pam that a visit to Aunt Margaret might be a good idea. I had never met the lady, and I was certain she was not aware of Gere's actions. Margaret was a Quaker lady, very quiet and poorly informed about her affairs. Also, she was not at all fond of Gere. Together, we told Margaret about the mismanagement. Pam offered to take charge and set things right, if Margaret would vote her shares with Pam instead of Gere. She immediately agreed, and we brought in my attorney, Marty Katz, to advise us. Needless to say, Gere was furious at being deposed. But the die was cast. Henceforth, Pam would be running Margaret's affairs, with guidance from Marty, and help from me. We also replaced the crooked accountant, who had been investing Margaret's money for his own benefit.

We breathed a sigh of relief, delighted to no longer be under Gere's thumb. However, we now had an angry enemy who we had deprived of her piggy bank!

We set about selling the inner city properties, and reinvesting the proceeds. Land around PBPCC was a hot commodity, and I was the resident expert. Margaret doubled her money on several parcels. Her other assets turned out to be major money. I never knew, nor did I ask exactly how much was involved, but it was well into seven figures. Margaret was most appreciative of Pam's performance, and eventually gave Pam power of attorney, and changed her will, making Pam the main beneficiary. At this point, Pam became independent of Gere, and set for life. All she had to do was keep Margaret happy, which meant our driving down for frequent visits. Margaret was a plain, simple person, not given to extravagance. I cautioned Pam about the importance of appearances, dressing plainly with little or no makeup for our visits. Also, it would not be advisable to be seen too often in the social pages at big Palm Beach parties.

We were expecting our only child, so we were pretty low key for a while. Eventually, Pam believed she could get away with high living on the party circuit without offending Margaret. I reminded her that Gere would, at every opportunity, point out to Margaret that Pam was living a flashy lifestyle, using Margaret's money.

After our son, William Charles Parry Elebash (named after Pam's father), was born, Pam gradually began to live it up, running around with Cornelia Guest, getting her picture in the paper at every party, and wearing the latest cutting edge outfits. Instead of the calm and reserved person I married, she had become a real party animal. She totally disregarded my advice.

When LeGrand and Palmer came for a visit, she treated them badly, and told me they should no longer be part of our life. For me, this was a deal breaker. Under no circumstances was I going to abandon my children. Our marriage began to unravel, and it was not long before we divorced. Pam thought she was fixed for life with Margaret's fortune, and she no longer needed me to help her. It was truly a horror show. How could I have been such a poor judge of a person's character? I had made a big mistake getting into this marriage, and now had an infant son to boot.

Settling our affairs was not difficult as I did not want anything from her. I just wanted out, I wanted visitation rights with Billy, and I wanted her to change her name back to Parry. We had been married about three years. I was back to life as a single man, and I was able to restore my relationship with LeGrand and Palmer.

NEW OPPORTUNITY

While all this was going on, my business continued to thrive at PBPCC. The polo community was growing by leaps and bounds, and I was getting the lion's share of the customers. One of my clients was Peter Brant from Greenwich, Connecticut. Ten years my junior, he was a very successful entrepreneur. Peter and his cousin, Joe Allen, were the general partners in two newsprint mills, one in Canada and the other in Virginia. The limited partners were the *Washington Post* and The Dow Jones Group, publishers of the *Wall Street Journal*. He also was one of the major collectors of contemporary art and a breeder of race horses. He had recently acquired a large tract of land, approximately 1,500 acres, in the back country of Greenwich, known as the Rosenstiel Property. He planned to develop an exclusive residential community, minimum lot size ten acres, with polo fields. He approached me about becoming the sales/marketing person, requiring me to spend the summer months in Greenwich. Being in Florida at PBPCC in the winter was a plus as it would allow me to be in contact with the polo clientele, our target audience for Conyers Farm, as the development would be known.

We quickly reached an agreement regarding compensation and the assignment started immediately.

I still had my PBPCC operation, and now this project would vault me to a new financial level.

One day, I received a call from Sam Webb Jr., the son of cousin LeGrand's best friend. Sammy and I had been friends at Yale, and we also shot birds together after college. He told me that LeGrand really missed me, and would I please call him to reconnect. I thought LeGrand had probably heard of my success in real estate, and wanted to see if there was some way he might benefit from that. Even though he had been a serious thorn in my side in my adult life, he was responsible for launching me at Choate and Yale. Then again, he had said to me many years ago, "If it weren't for me, you would be pumping gas in a filling station in Florence." So, I placed the call. His first words were, "I have missed you more than you can imagine."

At this point, LeGrand was married to Katherine, one of the ladies he had seen during his troubles. They were happy, settled in Columbus, and spending the summer in Dorset, Vermont. He was still a member of Okeetee, and spent time there during the shooting season. I invited him to visit me at PBPCC, where I was renting a townhouse after splitting with Pam. It was a nice visit, and I actually felt sorry for him. He was showing his age, and short on funds to cover Okeetee expenses. Inflation had eroded his purchasing power, but he was still trying to keep up the lifestyle.

Over the next few days, I tried to assess the totality of LeGrand's impact on my life. No doubt he set me on a very special track when he plucked me out of Coffee High School in Florence and sent me to Choate. Absent that event, there is no way to possibly judge what I may have done with my life, or where I might be today. In spite of the troubles, there was much that was good and beneficial from my relationship with him, and I began to catalogue these things.

Under his influence, I gave up smoking, adopted a rigorous exercise program, embarked on a continuing education program, changed my diet to better conform with the latest health advice, learned to ride horses and shoot a shotgun, thereby enjoying the experience of foxhunting in Ireland and shooting quail, doves, and ducks plantation style in south Alabama and at the Okeetee Club in Ridgeland, South Carolina, traveled to St. Moritz to ski, visited Milan, Italy, via chartered plane to see the opera, joined the Racquet & Tennis Club in New York City, learned to play court tennis, visited Newport, Rhode Island, where I played on the grass courts with Jimmy Van Allen, the inventor of the tiebreak scoring system in tennis, and met scores of interesting people from the UK, Texas, and New York.

As I reflected on my life with LeGrand, I made the decision to not only reconnect, but to use my resources to enhance his twilight years. I entertained him, and Katherine, in Palm Beach and New York, always picking up the check. I also made an arrangement with him regarding Okeetee. In exchange for regular visits to the club with him, I began covering all costs for the bird dogs. This made a huge difference in his life, as he could now afford to use the club more often. Later, I made a deal with a friend of mine in Augusta, Georgia, to share the string of bird dogs. Billy Morris owned a collection of newspapers, and had acquired one of the finest quail plantations in the south, Wade Plantation, about an hour's drive south of Augusta. I met Billy through my connection with Peter Brant's newsprint company. The dogs were stationed at Wade Plantation under the watchful eyes of Billy's manager, and Billy paid the regular expenses. He only hunted on weekends because he was a full-time business executive. Therefore, LeGrand and I scheduled our Okeetee visits for midweek. We would pick up the dogs on a Tuesday, use them at Okeetee, and return them for Billy's use on the weekend. Initially, we pooled the dogs we both owned, and going forward I would occasionally buy additional dogs as needed. Good bird dogs were selling for $500 to $1,000 per copy, but we only added about two each year, as older dogs were retired. This was a very efficient arrangement, and worked to everyone's satisfaction. Occasionally, we would host Billy and his wife, Sissie, at Okeetee, and he would reciprocate by inviting us to shoot with him at Wade.

MORE OPPORTUNITY: BEAR ISLAND PAPER COMPANY

My work with Peter Brant was going great. We were selling home sites at Conyers Farm, and I had devised a marketing plan that worked perfectly. I acted as the owner's agent, and offered a full buyer's broker commission to any agent who delivered a buyer into my hands. Usually agents shy away from selling lots in an undeveloped subdivision, because it takes too much effort on their part to learn everything they needed to know to handle a buyer—just finding the lot lines could be a challenge, much less understanding the covenants, restrictions, building regulations, environmental issues, etc. Many Greenwich brokers refused to cooperate with us because one of their own did not control the listing and we were not in the multiple listing service. However, I quickly found a local broker who had the vision to see the potential opportunity available here, and the eventual future business that could result from re-sales and referrals. Brad Hvolbeck was a Greenwich native and had owned his brokerage firm for many years. Soon, he was responsible for delivering the majority of our buyers. Also, Matt Matthews, who owned a homebuilding firm specializing in high-end properties, became interested in Conyers Farm, and consequently built the majority of the homes. Both of these fellows were a big reason we were so successful in our sales operation. If we had a prospective buyer, we would immediately introduce them to Matt, who could guide them through the construction process and the maze of regulations imposed by the Town of Greenwich. It was a good deal for all concerned, and Peter Brant was happy with the rate of sales, and the steady increase in sale prices.

By being in Peter's office, I began to learn about the newsprint business. Newsprint is the single largest cost in producing a newspaper. All paper mills are capital intensive, so guaranteed contracts were important. There was a continual tug of war between the producers and the publishers. The pricing system created this battle as the producers wanted long-term contracts at fixed prices, while the publishers wanted flexible pricing so as to take advantage of excess supply situations. Bear Island was a relatively new mill, and it was using a new process to make newsprint that used fewer chemicals, hence it was better from an environmental viewpoint. However, it was not as resistant to tearing while on the press. But it also was a brighter color and produced a better looking product. Bear Island was having trouble selling its paper, because older mills had existing contracts with all the major publishers, who were reluctant to change suppliers.

Overhearing a discussion between Peter and his partner, Joe Allen, regarding the inability of his salespeople to pry business away from the old boy network, I suggested that perhaps they were not approaching the publishers' buyers the right way. They looked at each other, and said, "Why don't you give it a try? You are a Southerner and maybe speak the language better with the southern publishers."

I answered, "I don't know anything about this business. I just recently learned that newsprint was the big rolls of paper used on the big printing presses!"

They gave me the directory of all the publishers in the US, and said to look it over and see if I thought I might be able to gain entry somewhere. I quickly learned that about ten companies owned 90 percent of the newspapers in the US.

While shooting quail with LeGrand, I met other shooters, one of whom was Jim Kennedy, the son of one of the Cox sisters who owned the *Atlanta Journal Constitution* and a number of other papers. His family owned Clarendon Plantation in Beaufort, South Carolina, and Jimmy had converted it from a cattle operation to one of the finest quail plantations in the south. Jimmy was not the newsprint buyer for his company, but I thought the connection might come in handy, if I did not use it to gain an audience with his buyer.

The Southern Newspaper Publishers Association held an annual meeting in Boca Raton, and all the southern publishers attended. Also in attendance were all the salesmen representing every newsprint producer in the US. I was sent to the meeting, my mission being to meet, and get an appointment with the Cox buyer, Carl Gross. Not only was he the buyer, he was a long-time board member and close friend of the Cox family. I found him on the practice putting green after lunch, about to play a round of golf with two newsprint sales reps. I introduced myself, and requested an appointment with him in Atlanta the following week. He said, "Well, if you are going to tell me the same thing I am hearing from other salesmen, you are wasting your time." I asked for ten minutes next week, and he agreed to the meeting. Peter and Joe were glad to receive this news, but not very optimistic. Nonetheless, I thought it was worth the trip.

I did not ask Peter for guidance, because I knew that he had the same view shared by all the other mill owners, i.e., long-term contracts at a fixed price. My plan was to see what terms would get us into the Cox pressroom. Peter might turn it down, but the old pitch was not working so I was willing to go way outside the box if it would give us a chance to become one of his suppliers.

When I walked into his office, I immediately said, "Carl, you buy tons of paper every year, and we have a mill nearby in Ashland, Virginia. There must be some way we can do business. And by the way, I don't know anything about newsprint—I just recently learned that it was the paper on which newspapers are printed."

He responded, "Well, that is a unique approach. Basically, I don't like the way newsprint is priced. I do not want to sign contracts at fixed prices for years."

I said, "What if we change that? Suppose Bear Island would give you flexible pricing. We can adjust to market conditions every six months, or three months, or weekly. Also, we can back the freight out of the price, and deal with it separately. Neither of us make money on freight charges, so it does not make sense for it to be the same, regardless of where the paper is coming from. We have a relatively cheap rate coming from Virginia, as opposed to your Canadian suppliers."

I could see him thinking. This pricing issue is a double-edge sword. The shorter the adjustment period, the more danger there was for both sides, depending which way the market, known as the "spot price," moved. He said he would consider a deal with a six-month adjustment period. I asked if we agreed to that, would he give us an order for 12,000 tons per year, with the right to cancel if we disagreed on the adjustment, or at the end of each calendar year. He answered in the affirmative. I told him he would have an answer in forty-eight hours.

"You did what?" Peter exclaimed.

I said, "Do you want the order or not? It is the only chance you have to become one of Cox's main suppliers."

After consulting with Joe, they agreed and a deal was signed. Newsprint pricing would never be the same again. Quickly, I went to several other publishers with the same message, and received several more orders. Before the old line producers knew what hit them, we had taken business away from them. It did not take long for flexible pricing to become the norm. Basically, newsprint is a commodity. Fixed pricing was as out of date as horse and buggy transportation. Peter and Joe chuckled when they told me, "You better watch your back. Those other salesmen may put out a contract on you." Adding this new role in newsprint to my business activities, I could more easily afford to upgrade my string of polo ponies.

BEAR ISLAND
TIMBERLANDS

A few years later, Peter brought up the subject of the timberland owned by Bear Island. Did he really need to own 300,000 acres of timberland to guarantee a steady supply of wood chips to the mill? Approximately half of Virginia's timberlands belonged to large wood products companies. The other half was owned by individuals, and two hundred acres was considered a large individual holding. The advantage of being a major owner was that, if pulp prices rose, you could harvest more from your own land, and if they fell, you could buy from others. Safe? Yes. Economically attractive? No.

Timberland is a good investment for large pension funds with very long horizons. If you let the trees grow to full maturity, the return is much greater than the short time frame. Also, there is a steady flow of pulp wood into the marketplace. Your cost may vary but you can always obtain pulp wood. Even large owners regularly thinned their timber stands to allow space for trees to grow larger and to sell pulp wood.

Peter and the partners could generate much greater returns by investing in their core businesses, as opposed to holding on to a long-term investment in pine forests. So, I was asked to come up with a sales plan. The woodlands manager was also asked for a plan. In a meeting with the partners, the woodlands manager presented his plan first: select the parcels you want to sell, hold an auction, and cash on the spot from the high bidder. I proposed that we not identify parcels, but go where the market takes us. I wanted thirty days to tour the 838 parcels spread across thirty-eight counties in Virginia. Then, I would contact every law firm, bank, and developer in the state with a simple message: Bear Island wants to reduce its land inventory. If you are interested, please call me to identify what exactly you might be interested in. We would negotiate from that point. Not all land is equal, in either timber value or location value. I wanted the flexibility to sell any parcel if the price was right. This was, of course, anathema to the woodlands manager, because he wanted to protect the best timberland from sale. To quote Hillary Clinton, I said, "What difference does it make?" The object should be to maximize the amount received regardless of the timber stand, which could be accounted for in the price. The manager anticipated an average sale price of approximately $800 per acre. I thought my plan would easily exceed his number. The partners gave me the assignment.

On my inspection tour, the woodland employee assigned to me, Bob Doyon, kept asking me, "Don't you want to walk the land?" No, I said. I was more interested in the location, how far from towns or major roads.

I could see from the topo maps all I needed to know about the land itself. So, a "drive by" was all I needed.

After the tour, I returned to Greenwich, armed with a location map showing every parcel, all 838 of them. I then began contacting every law firm, bank, and developer in Virginia, notifying them that Bear Island was a seller and to call if they were interested. The first few calls came in, and the caller wanted to know which parcels in, say, Dinwiddie County, we wanted to sell? My answer was always the same. "How do I know? I could study that county for ten years and not know as much as you do right now. If you want to look, I will send Bob Doyon out with you to look at any and all parcels in your area of interest. If you see something you want to buy, tell me about your development plan, show me the numbers you are projecting and tell me what you can afford to pay for the land if we give you a free option ($1000 refundable deposit) for six months while you get approvals. Then and only then do you close on the deal. We will even consider a small amount of bridge financing, if we are totally secured. One more thing, I come from a development background. I will vet your proposal, and if you are offering me a fair price, we will sell. If you are trying to low ball me, I will not talk to you again."

It did not take long for this message to spread throughout the state. More than one person told me, "We have *never* heard of a paper or timber company who would do this kind of deal." I explained that my goal was to maximize the net proceeds from land sales for my clients and by giving the option, a buyer should be able to pay more than he would if he had to take the immediate risk without knowing he could develop the land as planned.

Over a ten-year period, I greatly reduced the acreage owned by Bear Island, at an average price of over $1800 per acre. My clients were happy, and I was happy. My financial position had increased in quantum leaps. Altogether, I was spending the majority of my time on Peter Brant–related ventures. Is this a long way from College Park, Florence, and Columbus, or what?

GREENWICH
POLO CLUB

Greenwich Polo Club was a goal, perhaps a dream, of Peter's. Before PBPCC, he had taken up polo, playing at the Fairfield Hunt Club and a few other venues close to his home in Greenwich. Peter was, and remains, one of the most talented, smart, and committed individuals I have ever met. His family had a thriving paper business, but he took it to an entirely different level. After attending the University of Colorado, he looked at his family's paper business, and concluded that the real money was to be made in owning the production part of the paper business. Instead of being a middleman, converting newsprint rolls to school tablets and other products, he correctly determined that the most profitable route was to own the mills that produced the paper. He put together the partnership with the Dow Jones Company to buy a bankrupt mill in Canada. Dow Jones would buy, for their own consumption, a significant percentage of the newsprint produced, and the balance would be sold to other publishers. Market timing was perfect, as newsprint prices rose in the next few years. Based on this success, he then brought the

Dow Jones and *Washington Post* together to build a new mill in Ashland, Virginia. Meanwhile, he was becoming one of the main collectors of contemporary art. He also saw an opportunity to own an important piece of land in the back country of Greenwich adjacent to his home property, White Birch Farm. The property was being offered for sale by the estate of Lewis Rosenstiel who had acquired it in the 1930s. For years, the property, 1,500 acres more or less, had laid fallow, no development, buildings left in disrepair, roofs ripped off to avoid paying property taxes, and orchards becoming overgrown. Mr. Rosenstiel had attempted to get approval for a high-density project for middle-class homes. When that effort failed, he simply let nature take its course.

When it was offered for sale, there were several potential buyers, but they wanted to make purchase subject to approval for development by the Greenwich town authorities. Peter stepped in and agreed to buy with no approval contingencies. He believed that he could get approvals necessary for a low density residential plan.

When I met Peter at PBPCC in the early eighties, he was in the process of seeking approvals for what would become Conyers Farm. It was at this time that he offered me the position as his sales/marketing man. I had sold Peter a condominium on Polo Island, and a parcel of land for a polo barn. He partnered with Henryk de Kwiatkowski to buy eighty acres which they would split fifty-fifty for their two barns. Peter was asked at some point, "Why did you choose Elebash for the Conyers Farm position?"

He replied, "Because he sold me property I really did not want, so I figured he could sell Conyers Farm lots as well!"

Selling lots was just part of the assignment. Peter wanted to create the one and only first-class polo venue on the East Coast. We were able to get a few "bell cows" to buy immediately. Peter Orthwein bought two lots and Geoffrey Kent bought the "show home" that had been built on spec. Soon we had other key players—Mickey Tarnopol, Henryk, and George Lindeman, whose youngest son was just taking up polo—buying lots and joining the Greenwich Polo Club.

Personally, my polo was improving as a result of playing, and just hanging around with these people. Soon I was playing in eighteen- to twenty-goal events, making a team by partnering with another lowly rated player/patron. If we both hired a pro rated at 8 goals or more, we could compete. As an analogy from tennis, if I hire John McEnroe and you hire Pete Sampras, we can play a doubles match.

At GPC, we were able to field four to six teams of this level for the months of June and July. We would then move to Saratoga for polo in August. Several of our patrons (playing team sponsors) were involved in the horse racing world, and Saratoga was the place to be in August. We exercised the polo ponies in the morning, went to the races in the afternoon, and played our polo matches at 6:00 p.m. Nice way to spend the month of August. Back at PBPCC, it was, as always, a hot and muggy summer.

My routine was to leave south Florida in May, haul the ponies to Greenwich, then to Saratoga for August, then back to Greenwich for a few weeks before heading back south. Yes, I was working, but I was having a ball playing polo with some of the best players in the world. Peter Brant had Gonzalo Pieres, then considered the best player in the world and rated 10 goals, plus Hector Barrantes at 7 goals, but always considered to be among the best players and a superb judge of horseflesh. Hector ran Peter's barn, and deserves much credit for the quality of the White Birch ponies. My hired guns were Ernesto Trotz, Julian Hipwood, and Benjamin Araya, at various times.

To promote interest, and spectators, at GPC, we set up a program whereby charitable organizations could host a benefit luncheon fieldside during Sunday polo matches. This concept had worked at PBPCC, and in Greenwich it literally caught fire. The polo club furnished a barebones party tent, charged a "site fee," and the charity did the rest. These events were very elegant from the beginning. Benefactors paid for caterers, etc., and tickets were in high demand. GPC became *the* place to be and to be seen on Sundays in June and July. Being close to New York, and having a high demographic audience in the neighborhood, these luncheon events became major moneymakers for the charities. Paul Newman's Hole-in-the-Wall Gang still puts on their event in June, and clears over $500,000 every year. Matches are always well attended as the caliber of polo is very good. Recently, Prince Harry participated in an event.

It was the mid eighties, and I was dividing my time between Greenwich and Palm Beach. I owned a polo villa at PBPCC, which I eventually shared with my college roommate and best friend, Larry Downs. Larry was a psychiatrist, living in New Hampshire but practicing in New York City. I was renting a large home in Greenwich which allowed me to have my three children visit often. LeGrand was at St. Paul's School in Concord, New Hampshire, and Palmer was about to enroll at Choate–Rosemary in Wallingford, Connecticut. It happened that both her father (me) and her stepfather (John Rivers) were Choate graduates. Somewhere along the line, Choate had gone co-ed. By 1985, most of the prestigious prep schools had converted from all boys to co-ed.

A few years before I rented the Greenwich house on a yearly basis, I had rented, for the summer season, a beautiful townhome on 93rd Street in Manhattan, between Park Avenue and Madison Avenue. A Racquet Club buddy, Eddie Ulmann, had acquired it during the time when New York City appeared to be on the verge of bankruptcy. It was one of three homes on the block that once belonged to members of the George Baker family. Eddie bought it at the bottom of the NYC market, for the princely sum of $370,000 or thereabouts. Rather than let it sit empty for the summer months, he rented it to me for $5,000 per month. It came equipped with a housekeeper, and a butler was available on call. This is a five-story mansion—kitchen in the basement with a dumbwaiter to bring meals up to the dining room on the ground floor, large entrance hall, majestic staircase leading to the second floor which was a rabbit's warren of bedrooms and baths for servants or children, an elevator serving all the upper floors, grand living room, library, guest rooms, and a mammoth master suite on the third and fourth floors. It was truly a magnificent living arrangement.

I invited all three of my kids to spend the summer with me in New York. To watch over the house and young occupants, I hired a girl who was a Yale senior, and also a member of the Book & Snake senior society. When Yale went co-ed, most senior societies quickly followed. Billy was enrolled at a day camp in the neighborhood, and she would walk him there every morning, and back late afternoon. Palmer invited one of her Charleston girlfriends to visit, and I engaged a driver/bodyguard to take the girls anywhere they wanted to go. Among other activities, they were taking ballet lessons. LeGrand was old enough to go out on his own, and he was frequenting the jazz clubs. He had taken up drums, and played with a group at St. Paul's. I would drive out to Greenwich most days and return before dark. This was a summer to be remembered for a long time.

Needless to say, I enjoyed a very active social life that summer. Eddie's home was the ultimate "babe trap!" I hosted the occasional dinner party, and remember one time when both Gene Scott and Billy Talbert were among the guests.

NEW YORK CITY AND GREENWICH

During the next winter polo season at PBPCC, I noticed that my Florida real estate sales were tapering off. In the early eighties, there was a huge rush of buyers getting in on the ground floor, but now it was more like a slow but steady stream. As always happens, when real estate sales heat up, the ranks of sales associates swell accordingly. One day after a polo game, my groom told me, "Guess what, Peter, I am getting my real estate license!" From this point on, I would devote more time to the Brant interests, where I controlled the inventory of lots at Conyers Farm, and was in the middle of the Bear Island land sales program. My sales at PBPCC were no longer as important to me as they once were. I would take what I could get, but the die was cast. More agents meant fewer sales per agent. In most real estate markets, 90 percent of the deals are made by 10 percent of the agents. New agents in and around PBPCC were at it seven days a week, and I had other, more profitable interests taking up more than half of my time.

Spending more time in Greenwich, where I now was renting a nice home, suited me, as both LeGrand

and Palmer were now in prep school. I could visit them regularly as it was a short drive to Choate, and even though the drive to St. Paul's was longer, it was not difficult for a relatively young, fit adult. After St. Paul's, LeGrand went to Yale, and this was super convenient for me. He was on the varsity heavyweight crew, and I hardly ever missed a home meet. It was a real pleasure to drive up to New Haven, and take him and a few crew mates to dinner at Mory's. These boys had already wolfed down a full meal back in their college, but as oarsmen, their appetites were insatiable. Steaks for all, please! One year the crew team was invited to tour China and teach rowing to young people. This was possible because one of my Yale classmates, Winston Lord, was the current ambassador to China. Winston was a career diplomat, and was the architect of China policy for four presidents. He is also married to a Chinese lady, which did not diminish his status.

Senior year, LeGrand was tapped into Book & Snake, and I really enjoyed meeting and visiting with his delegation, now eight men and eight women. Palmer was graduating from Choate–Rosemary and headed to Brown University in Providence, Rhode Island. She had excelled at Choate and certainly would have been accepted at Yale. However, when the subject was broached, she said, "Too many Elebashes have gone to Yale. I want to try a different route." Many of her Choate friends were attending Brown, so it was very appealing to her.

Billy was visiting me in Greenwich during school vacations and made some friends there. Among those were the Brant triplets. I remember throwing a party for the gang, and hiring an entertainer who brought a trained chimpanzee, who played with the kids, performed on roller skates, and painted pictures that actually looked like they could have been painted by a human.

Meanwhile, I continued to date a succession of ladies. This time, I told myself, I will be extremely careful before making any permanent arrangement. And I was firmly against having any more children. To guarantee that would not happen, I had a vasectomy. By the third date, my female friends were apprised of my condition. Ideally, I thought the best course would be to marry a woman who already had children, and given the soaring divorce rate, there were plenty of prospects. For men and women, there is merit in selecting a new mate who was already experienced with the trials and tribulations that inevitably arise in married life, as well as the pleasures.

I was still playing polo, and shooting at Okeetee with cousin LeGrand. I met some fabulous ladies, who I will not mention by name. They ranged from Park Avenue socialites to midwestern girls working in and around New York. I was in no hurry to marry again, but I felt I would eventually want the right life partner. The trick, as always, is finding the "right one." Peter Brant's father, Murray, told me, "Picking a wife is like reaching in a bag and trying to pull out a snake without getting bitten!" He was a very interesting man, a first-generation immigrant. Regarding work, he would say, "My footsteps were the first ones in the snow every morning!" I could always tell when Murray was in the office, because most of the lights would be turned off. He knew the value of hard work and frugality.

DISTURBING NEWS

Somewhere along this timeline, when I was enjoying a few days at the Okeetee Club, I received an urgent call from Pam Parry. The fear in her voice was palpable. She had just learned that Aunt Margaret had paid a visit to Marty Katz at his office in West Palm Beach. Margaret wanted to revoke Pam's power of attorney, remove her from the will, and fire her immediately. As I had predicted, Gere had been feeding Margaret a steady stream of reports of Pam's extravagant lifestyle in Palm Beach. Pam's half brother, Charles Parry, had joined Margaret at this meeting. I had only learned of the existence of a half brother about the time Pam was taking over the management of Margaret's affairs. Charles was the issue from an encounter between Pam's father and a lady in the neighborhood. My advice to Pam was to come clean, cooperate fully, and throw herself on Margaret's mercy. Perhaps she could negotiate a deal whereby she could keep some assets in recognition of her performance as financial manager. Pam did not follow my advice, hence starting a protracted legal action that would last for years.

My main concern was the well-being of Billy, and it was unaffected for the time being. Pam had a full-time nanny, and Billy was beginning school. I did not receive any updates from Pam, so I put it out of my mind for the time being. It would be a few years before the rubber would meet the road.

Among the attractive ladies coming into my life was Dorsey Waxter, the director of a prestigious art gallery in midtown Manhattan. We quickly became an item, and romance was in the air. Dorsey had never been married. I was breaking one of my rules, i.e., form a relationship with a previously married woman who had children about the same age as mine. As the relationship progressed, she became aware of the fact that I had taken the ultimate action to rule out having any more children. After many discussions, she decided that this was not a deal breaker for her. However, we did stop seeing each other for unrelated reasons. She sensed that I was getting cold feet, so she decided to continue searching for someone who was fully committed to marriage. About six months later, I had second thoughts, and called her up. She informed me that she was in a relationship. So, I told her to let me know if it did not last. I would call her occasionally, just to check in and confirm my interest in giving it another try if and when she was available. Eventually, that relationship failed, and we started seeing each other again. She was, quite correctly, wary, so things proceeded slowly.

When I finally popped the question, she accepted, and we were married in her hometown of Easton, Maryland. All three of my children attended the ceremony, as did cousin LeGrand. Dorsey was proving to be an excellent stepmother. Initially, we continued to live in my rented house in Greenwich, but spent some nights in her apartment in lower Manhattan. Later, we rented an apartment on the Upper East Side, making my commute to Greenwich much easier. Dorsey also owned a small home in Millbrook, New York, which is about ninety miles north of the city, up the Taconic State Parkway. I had friends in Millbrook, and was starting to play polo there as I began phasing out of high goal polo in Greenwich and at PBPCC. Frankly, the sport was becoming fiercely expensive, way more than I was willing, or able, to cover. Millbrook polo was low goal, so the cost of the "hired guns" was a fraction of the cost in the high goal world.

Ultimately, we decided to move to Millbrook. We would give up the rental home in Greenwich, keep the New York apartment, and replace Dorsey's Millbrook home with something much larger. We found the perfect place, a country home on ten acres, on Tower Hill Road which was in the hunt country (meaning the foxhounds territory).

I had been checking in with Pam periodically, to get reports on Billy's situation and activities. I was assured by Pam that all was well in Palm Beach. She barely mentioned the altercation with Margaret, so I assumed she had settled. Soon I tried to call Pam and got no answer. I finally called Marty Katz to find out what, if anything, was going on. The story left me speechless. Pam was defying a court order to turn over some bearer bonds, and the sheriff was trying to locate her. I immediately went to Palm Beach, and found Billy living with the nanny in West Palm Beach. Pam had been arrested, spent a night in the county jail, and was bailed out by her mother the next day.

It was necessary for Billy to move in with me and Dorsey. Fortunately, Dorsey, my wife of only a few months, was totally agreeable about this, knowing that I really had no choice. I persuaded the nanny, Ina Mussenden, to move to Millbrook, and be a live-in nanny/housekeeper to Billy, who was now in the second grade. Our add-on plans for the Tower Hill home were slightly modified to create an apartment for Ina. I don't know what I would have done if Ina had not come with Billy. This was God at work in our lives.

The move went smoothly, and Billy entered school at Dutchess Day, an excellent private school in Millbrook.

As I contemplated the state of affairs, I realized that Dorsey was a stepmother with no chance to be a mother herself. I swallowed hard, and told her that under the new circumstances, I would be willing to undergo reversal surgery so we could have a child. The doctor who performed this procedure said his success rate was 95 percent. I became part of that 5 percent on which the reversal did not work. Disappointing for Dorsey, but a relief for me. We settled down in Millbrook, enjoying country living even though we, like many of our friends, were commuters.

I was doing well financially with Peter Brant's business, and we began to feel the strain of commuting to New York for Dorsey's business. She had a substantial salary from the gallery, but after taxes, it did not contribute enough to our bottom line to cover the cost of an apartment in the city. We essentially were spinning our wheels. The ultimate solution was for Dorsey to leave the gallery and start her own art advisory service, operating out of our home on Tower Hill Road. For overnights in New York, we used the River Club. I played tennis there, and they had hotel rooms. Dorsey had a strong client base, so she continued to produce significant income, and we could spend more time in Millbrook.

I had been agonizing over the failed reversal attempt, and trying to come up with some way to compensate for it. Dorsey loved to ride, and most of her friends had horses and were members of the Millbrook Foxhounds. I suggested we get her a horse so she no longer needed to borrow from a friend if she wanted to go on a trail ride. She was thrilled! Having had years of experience with horses, I definitely wanted this horse to be a sound jumper and have a good disposition. We went shopping in Middleburg, Virginia, where we met Eve Fout, an expert rider and excellent judge of horseflesh. She had the perfect horse in her barn. After one ride we knew this was the right animal for Dorsey. The price was $25,000. This would be the most expensive horse in the Millbrook Hunt field at the time, but safety was paramount.

Dorsey became a very good horsewoman and was taking lessons from the best instructors available. Soon she would be going to horse shows all over New England. Several years later, she would come within a fraction of a second of winning the main event for adult jumpers at the South Hampton Classic. By then, we had "traded up" to a much more expensive horse, which we purchased at the PBPCC horseshow.

I was considering retiring from polo, not only because of the rapidly escalating cost but also for safety reasons. In the past several years, more players my age were getting seriously injured. Norman Brinker fell in a high goal practice game and was partially paralyzed. He had been very fit, and was rated 3 goals, which put him among the top 200 players in the US. After the accident, he was a shadow of his former self, and looked as if he had aged by twenty-five years. As you already heard, Peter Schuster, a German with whom I fielded a team, fell in Berlin, and only partially recovered over a two-year period. He later died as the result of a fall at PBPCC. Polo is a dangerous sport. It's like "hockey on horseback," definitely a sport for youngsters. In the past three years, there have been three fatalities at PBPCC. Skeeter Johnston, son of Skee and a 3 goal player, had a bad fall, and died within hours. Tracy Mactaggart had a freak accident and was unplugged three days later. This year, Carlos Gracida, formally a 10 goal player, was killed when his horse fell on him. There were more examples of why it would be wise for me to hang it up, at least a dozen more accidents ending with varying levels of paralysis. So, I decided this would be my last season of polo.

About that time, Gary Beller and I teamed up with the two Bostwick boys, Ricky and Charlie, for the annual Eddie Moore twelve-goal tournament at Millbrook Polo Club. Their father, Pete Bostwick, was one of the legendary players from the early days of polo on Long Island and had carried a 9 goal rating at his peak. His boys began playing at an early age, and were now rated at 5 and 6 goals, respectively. More importantly, they owned only the best horses, which gave us a distinct advantage over the other teams. We won that event, but only after winning most of our games in overtime. I credit Bostwick's horses for the victory. This was a good time for me to retire, and spend more time shooting at the Tamarack Club. Henceforth, my equestrian activity would be confined to hanging on the rail watching Dorsey go around the jumping course. I had plenty of company, as most of my friends' wives were out there too.

Billy was doing well at Dutchess Day, or so I thought. By the time he hit sixth grade, we discovered that he was not comprehending math, yet he was being passed on to the next level and not getting the tutoring he needed. Considering the tuition cost, I was not at all happy about this. At a cocktail party, someone told us about the Eaglebrook School in Deerfield, Massachusetts. It is a pre-prep school with a sterling reputation for producing well-qualified candidates for the best prep schools. Note: my grandson, Hudson Elebash, the son of my oldest son, LeGrand, is graduating from Eaglebrook this year.

Within a week, we had driven up to check it out. If you Google Eaglebrook, you will see the most incredible school for boys in grades seven through nine. It would take many pages for me to adequately describe it, so I invite you to go to your computer. We enrolled

Billy to start the next year as a seventh grader. There was some trepidation, sending him to a boarding school at his age, but we could drive there in about two hours so we visited frequently.

With Billy away at school, Dorsey and I were empty nesters, except for Ina and our three dogs who were a constant source of amusement. Life in Millbrook was changing.

LIFE IN MILLBROOK

Dorsey continued with her riding, and I was doing a lot of shooting. We gave, and attended, many dinner parties, played tennis at the Millbrook Golf and Tennis Club, and became very active in our church, St. Peter's Episcopal, in Lithgow. I served on the vestry, and we ran the once-every-three-years auction, the main money source for the church. When I joined the vestry, I learned that the church owned 170 acres straddling the Millbrook–Amenia town line. It was a gift from Eliot Clarke to settle a tax dispute with Amenia. It was of no use to the church, and the church coffers were bare. I suggested we sell it and start an endowment fund. Much to my surprise, some church members objected violently, on no particular grounds. We finally overcame that hurdle, and I went to work studying the land and key issues, like how do we access it? We had no road frontage, but an access route had been identified at the time of the gift. There was a major problem, it was not possible to construct a driveway over the designated route as the terrain was way too steep. I began negotiations with Eliot, as he owned all the land over which we could build a driveway. To make a long story short, I determined a route that was possible, and would give Eliot as well as the church proper access to the top of the hill. I then solicited bids for the driveway and the low bid was $60,000. So I approached several church members to join me in co-signing a note at the bank to pay for the construction. Once we had a road, we would be able to sell the land and pay off the loan. Eliot would have, at no cost to him, a new way to access his high ground. The driveway would be jointly used. In forty-eight hours, I had ten commitments from endorsers, one of whom was Eliot. This was a great deal for him.

There were issues with the Dutchess Land Conservancy, because the then Director wanted such strict conservation easements that no one would want to buy our land. Once that was resolved, we began marketing the property. In the end, the buyer was the next-door neighbor, Chris Gallagher, who had no plans to develop it. This quieted the "antis" and the deal closed. St. Peter's now had, for the first time, an endowment of approximately $300,000. I think the value today is over $1,000,000.

The general real estate business in Millbrook was picking up. More people were buying second homes and prices were on the rise. My assignments with Peter Brant were going to run out soon, so I thought about entering the business in Millbrook. Previously, I did not think it would be worth the effort. Not enough high-value deals were being done to warrant the time and effort. Besides, Dorsey and I together were making all the money we really needed. The catalyst was Eliot

Clarke when he asked me to advise him on the possible sale of some of his land. Local brokers had been ineffective, so I agreed to study it. The land in question was across Highway 44 from the rest of his land, on which he had a historic home. Most of the other adjoining land belonged to the Millbrook School. I was already involved with the Dutchess Land Conservancy (DLC), and I was developing a strategy which I thought would help me with clients. Everett Cook had engaged me as a consultant to help him with easements on his three hundred plus acres. The idea was to prepare a "theoretical" subdivision plan which would maximize the value. Nobody actually wanted to subdivide, but if they could create tangible value by showing subdivided parcels which would sell at a higher price per acre than a large tract, the land owner could take a capital loss on their tax return equal to the difference between the value undivided rather than subdivided. For those in a high tax bracket, this was a substantial benefit. One could "monetize the asset" without selling land. By the same token, owners like Eliot could sell parcels with restrictions protecting his views, and realize a higher price per acre for fifty-acre parcels versus a three-hundred-acre parcel.

Working with the DLC, I prepared maps for Eliot's land, and put them on the market. Immediately, my phone began ringing, and the first caller was the Headmaster at the Millbrook School, Drew Casertano. They wanted a piece adjacent to their nature walk. Drew was interested in more of the land but did not have the money at the time. He and I met to discuss the schools land needs, and to identify parcels they owned but were not important in their overall plan. I had in mind possible land swaps which, with proper restrictions, would be beneficial to the school.

When all was said and done, I had sold all of Eliot's land at per-acre prices that astounded him, and I had found buyers for some dispensable school land, which provided funds for the school to buy additional land, some belonging to Eliot and some that was part of the Millbrook Equestrian Center (this was another deal I was working on at the same time). A very good start for me in the Millbrook market.

As a result of this success, I decided to open an office for The Elebash Company in downtown Millbrook.

THE HALCYON DAYS

The next few years were as good as it gets. We had many friends in Millbrook, and we all entertained each other with elegant dinner parties. We had built an addition to our home on Tower Hill Road, converting the former living room into a spacious dining room capable of comfortably seating twelve for dinner. We, as our friends did, served elegant meals with fine wines. If we were not hosting, we would usually be out several nights per week at friends' homes. Dorsey and the other wives were fully engaged in foxhunting and show jumping. Often, we would all travel to horseshows as far away as New Hampshire, where we men would cheer the girls on in their events, then go out on the town in the evening. These were usually three-day weekends. No problem for us—Billy was away at boarding school, Ina was keeping the homefront under control, walking daily with our three dogs, and our work schedules were flexible.

We went to France twice on biking excursions, with Eric and Dede Rosenfeld. They were avid bikers, and encouraged many in our circle to take rides around Millbrook on weekends, usually on back roads, lots of hills, distances about twenty miles. In France, we did not use Butterfield & Robinson, or any other guide service. We planned the entire route well in advance, faxed ahead for hotels and restaurants, and we took our bikes with us on Air France. Some disassembly was required, then they were packed in cardboard boxes and checked as baggage. Our clothes and personal items were packed in four saddlebags which hung over the bikes' wheels. Needless to say, this meant a careful selection of contents. However, we were able to carry all the clothing we needed for ten days on the road, including something appropriate for dining in a fancy restaurant. With good maps and a compass, we easily found our way around the French countryside, covering thirty to fifty miles per day. One time, as we were approaching a lunch destination in a country town, some of the restaurant staff were out in front of their establishment, looking down the road for the crazy Americans who had booked a reservation via fax a month ago.

My oldest son, LeGrand, married in 1995. After Yale, and a few months traveling the world, he had joined the Marines, gone to officer candidate school at Quantico, Virginia, then on to flight training. By 1995, he was flying a single seat F-18 fighter jet. His bride was Allison Barron, a graduate of the University of Alabama. The wedding was in the mountains of North Carolina, near Cashiers, where his stepfather had built a lovely club with croquet and tennis to go along with the fine dining. Dorsey and I were in attendance. Kathleen was running the show, and it was a grand affair. All of LeGrand's groomsmen were his friends from St. Paul's. He also organized a military "sword arch" made up of fellow F-18 pilots, dressed in snappy white uniforms. The actual service was held outdoors near the edge of a cliff which dropped down about a thousand feet to the valley floor. It was a beautiful, tranquil scene, until the final prayer was being intoned by the minister. Suddenly, a strange, loud noise was rapidly approaching the wedding party, coming along the leading edge of the cliff. Without telling LeGrand, his fellow pilots had arranged for one of their group to fly his practice mission right over the wedding party. The noise was deafening as the F-18 appeared just over the edge of the cliff, so it looked like he was only a hundred feet above the ground. He came back around, wiggled his wings, and was gone in an instant.

The reception went on well into the night, and a grand time was had by all. The next day, Dorsey and I stopped by a farm on our way to the airport to look at a horse being recommended by her trainer, Peter Leone, as a possible upgrade (we had already done the upgrade once before). No doubt this jumper could easily clear the four- to five-foot fences in the "high adult jumper" division, but Dorsey did not appear to be comfortable over these heights. The asking price was $150,000. I was not enthusiastic, but offered $100,000 which was summarily rejected. On the flight, I told Dorsey that I thought this show jumping business was getting a bit out of hand, way too expensive, like polo, for us to continue at this level. She seemed to understand, so that was the end of that.

Palmer graduated from Brown in 1993. She had the good fortune to secure a position with Goldman Sachs, where she spent two years before getting her MBA at Kellogg Business School in Chicago. From there, she worked for several companies before settling down at the Gap company headquarters in San Francisco. After a long string of very attractive suitors, she finally married Ethan Weiss on September 28, 2002. Ethan's family lives in Baltimore, Maryland. His father was, at the time, head of the cardiology department and on the admissions committee for Johns Hopkins Hospital. His mother was head of the music department at Peabody College. Ethan himself is a highly regarded research scientist at University of California San Francisco as well as a cardiologist. My friends in San Francisco tell me that Ethan and his team of research scientists are the brightest people they know. The wedding took place at Beaulieu Garden in the Napa Valley, a magical setting for a wedding and reception. Many of the extended families are former musicians, and at one point during the reception, with urging from Kathleen and Palmer, we descended en masse on the band stand. It was with some reluctance that the band members handed over their instruments to our clan, but they were pleasantly surprised to hear that we were, indeed, capable of making music. Ethan's mother, Susan, is a classical pianist and had no problem getting into a twelve-bar jazz tune, all improvised. Fortunately, I still had enough lip left to play the lead on a borrowed trumpet. LeGrand took over the drums while Kathleen's brother, Paul, played guitar. Ethan also played trumpet. Much to my surprise, we didn't sound all that bad. In fact, we got a round of applause when we sat down. Jane and I thoroughly enjoyed the entire weekend in Napa.

When Billy graduated from Eaglebrook, he went to the Kent School in Kent, Connecticut. The Headmaster, Dick Schell, was a friend of ours as he was often at Millbrook functions. Kent was only ten miles from Millbrook so we could visit with ease. Billy was a fourth former (tenth grader or sophomore), and adjusted well to prep school life. He played soccer in the fall, squash in the winter, and tennis in the spring. His tennis game was rapidly improving, and he was the best player at Kent at the time. He was just average in his studies, but this was no surprise as it had always been the case.

When spring vacation arrived, he wanted to go to the Bollettieri Tennis Academy in Bradenton, Florida, for a two-week course. After speaking with my old friend, Gene Scott, I agreed. Near the end of the camp, I visited the academy to see how Billy was progressing. In deference to Gene Scott, Nick himself performed a special evaluation test on him. The setting was a bit intimidating. On the stadium court were four of Nick's instructors, all big guys without shirts, wearing sunglasses and arms folded, stationed at the four corners of the court. At one end of the court stood another bruiser, with a hopper full of tennis balls and a racquet. Nick greeted Billy cordially, and placed him on the baseline. The balls started coming at a rapid pace, first forehands than backhands, all placed skillfully in Billy's "wheelhouse." Then he was moved to the net to hit volleys and overheads. It was over in about fifteen minutes, and Billy was exhausted!

Nick took me aside and said, "Peter, your boy could become a good player, but only if he immerses himself in tennis. No more soccer and squash, and to really be good, he should go to one of the academies." Nick would be happy to have him, but was quick to say there were several very good academies from which to choose.

Billy was begging me to let him leave Kent, come to Nick's and attend the school nearby where all the full timers studied. This was, to me, a radical plan. After much discussion with "team Billy," which included Dorsey and his mother Pam, Gene finally said to me, "Peter, do you really want to deny him what he perceives to be his life's dream? After all, if it doesn't work out, he can still go to college, and, after Nick's, he will always be one of the best tennis players wherever he lives." I agreed, and the deal was done. Gene had very kindly worked out a "barter deal" with Nick, thereby cutting about 25 percent off the astronomical tuition.

For the two years Billy was at the academy, Dorsey and I would visit often and participate in the weekly adult programs. We both improved our games, in addition to meeting some nice folks, particularly some of Nick's staff. Billy was improving in quantum leaps, and had moved up to the two groups just below the boys definitely going pro after leaving Nick. One day, I walked over to watch Billy's group, and he wasn't there. I was directed to a distant court, where he was hitting with a pre-teen Russian girl, who looked to be incredibly talented. Seems her father was commandeering Billy to be her regular hitting partner. His reason? He wanted her to face the toughest competition, and Billy was the only boy who did not object to hitting with a young girl. When I met the father, I learned that his daughter was Maria Sharapova. They had come to America with no money, so his daughter could learn tennis from the master, Nick Bollettieri. Her mother had stayed behind to care for the other children. Maria was the youngest student at Nick's and her dad was picking up any and all part time jobs to support his daughter.

Scroll forward to Wimbeldon several years later, and when I turned on the TV to watch the women's finals, there was Maria, putting a major beatdown on Serena Williams to win her first grand slam tournament. A small world, indeed!

Back in Millbrook, my real estate business was booming. A steady stream of young Wall Street financial types were buying second homes in the country, and Millbrook was a heavily favored location. Business was also good at Conyers Farm and in Virginia with Bear Island Timberlands. Dorsey's art business was good, but I began to think she preferred city life to the country, except on the weekends. Gradually, I perceived her becoming distant from me, spending more time with her girlfriends than with me. As this situation progressed, she was only happy and pleasant when we were with other people. When we were alone, she was quiet and melancholy.

From the beginning, we had enjoyed a robust love life. Until this happened, we would make time for intimacy several times a week. Our bedroom was very large, and had a fireplace with a small sitting area. It enjoyed a spectacular view in all four seasons, but a fire during the winter was particularly conducive to making love.

I tried to talk with her, find out what was bothering her, but she never opened up. Soon we were seeking marital counseling, but that did not change things. One day, the counselor told me, "I don't know if it is possible for you to turn this around. She is simply unhappy in the marriage." Very soon, there would be no more sex either. When pressed, she said, "I just can't do this anymore."

The halcyon days were over.

HERE WE GO AGAIN

To this day, I cannot completely understand why she wanted to leave and go back to New York. I would have done almost anything to continue the marriage, but was unable to strike any notes that appealed to her. I think the most likely answer is that she really missed being immersed in the contemporary art world—the people, the galleries, the auctions and private dealings appealed to her more than the prospect of continuing our way of life in Millbrook. She was a superior stepmother to Billy, and still keeps in touch with him to this day.

In short order, the Tower Hill home was sold but only because I agreed to lease it back for six months. We divided our assets and it was done. Now I was to learn what it meant to be living in Millbrook after getting divorced from a popular woman. No longer was I included in dinner parties, or even cocktail parties. The assumption, as expressed to me by some of these friends was, the man can go out and "cat around" but the poor woman needed nurturing. Dorsey continued to enjoy an active social life in Millbrook on the weekends, but I was persona non grata. So, at age sixty plus, I needed to start over, a depressing thought to say the least.

I bought a small antique home in Amenia, about fifteen miles from the center of Millbrook. There was a pool and a tennis court on this twenty-seven-acre spread. It was comfortable and cozy, but I was alone. If it wasn't for my hip pocket appeal, I probably would have had no social life at all during that time. However, I began to reach out in many directions. This was moderately successful, but not terribly satisfying. It also meant driving to the Bedford area or into New York City. For a single man, Millbrook was Deadsville.

At this point, I began to think about the meaning of life. What's the point? Are we simply born, live, and die, going into the earth from which we had come? I had always been connected to the Episcopal church, but I realized I was only a "cultural Christian," going through the motions on Sunday, but otherwise just trying to live a decent life following the Judeo-Christian ethic to the best of my ability as long as no sacrifice was required. I had recited the Apostles' Creed many times but the meaning of the words was lost on me.

The worst part of being stuck in Millbrook was the winters. The sun goes down about 4:00 p.m. and it is always cold. That's fine if you had a family, but being alone was very stressful. As my second winter there was approaching, I decided I must get away, spend some time soul searching, and decide what I was going to do with the rest of my life. I was absolutely burnt out with the succession of new women, and wanted to be alone to contemplate my future. Finally, I decided to rent a small, unpretentious apartment in Palm Beach on Brazilian Avenue, beginning in

January. I knew some people there, but did not reach out to them, as I was not looking for social activity. I wanted to be under the radar. I was delighted to be in a warm climate.

INTERLUDE

Now I want to scroll back to 1960, and talk about my life in the tennis world. As previously noted, my college friend Gene Scott gave me a tennis racquet, with the advice to practice, and learn from others who knew how the game was played. In Columbus, two of my friends were former college players at the University of Georgia. Joe Manderson and Charlie Bryant were my coaches and hitting partners. They would demonstrate the correct form and I would try to execute. Gradually, I developed a decent forehand, then backhand and volley. They would always play to my weakness so as to give me practice where needed. I was becoming a fair "club player" but was eager to keep improving.

Mainly, we played at the Green Island Country Club, which had a nice four-court setup. One court was in front of the tennis shop so spectators could sit on the porch to watch matches. One of our club members was Tom Molloy, a former ranked player in the days of Billy Talbert. He no longer played, but was keen to promote the tennis program by producing small events and tournaments for our amusement. He eventually moved away, to head up the Bay Point development in

Panama City. Most of the financial backing for Bay Point was coming from a few Columbus families. When Tom left, I inherited the mantle of tennis promoter at Green Island. We had previously discussed the possibility of staging a tournament with some of the top players in the US, but the idea had gone nowhere. This was the early sixties and all the major tournaments were amateur events. Jack Kramer had a pro tour that did not attract much attention, but some people followed the major Championships at Forest Hills, Wimbledon, Paris, and Australia, all of which did not allow the pros to compete. This would change in 1968 when the tennis authorities were dragged, kicking and screaming, into the modern era. My friend, Owen Williams, has written a fascinating book about that era. As the number one ranked player in South Africa in the 1950s and, briefly, tournament director at the US Open, he is an authority on the subject.

Some of our members began to push for some kind of event that would allow our club members to see, up close and personal, ranked players. Tennis was not on television back then. I mentioned that one of those players was my Yale friend, Gene Scott, who was a lawyer in New York but played in the Davis Cup and a few other tournaments. I agreed to call him. Basically, I thought we needed eight players for an event, and I planned on getting at least four of them from the highest ranked college players in the southeast. Gene called back in a few days with the following offer: For a fee of $6,000, he would bring Clark Graebner, currently ranked number 3 in the US, Gene himself ranked 10, and Herb Fitzgibbon ranked 15. I immediately thought about Mike Belkin, the top ranked player in Canada who had married a Columbus girl. Mike agreed to play for expenses as the fourth so the deal was set. Now I needed four good college players. I started at the top of the Southern Lawn Tennis Association's rankings, and began calling to extend invitations. All responses were the same—who else is playing? When I listed the nationally ranked fellows, every one of the college players quickly accepted the invitation. They wanted a shot at the big boys and this was their only opportunity in that day.

For a doubles event, I suggested to Gene that we pair the eight hired guns with the best club players. He agreed. I had no problem getting sponsors, as a requirement for participating in the pro-am doubles was that you be a sponsor. I think this was the first time a pro-am doubles event was offered in a tournament. We built box seating along the front of the tennis porch and quickly sold out. Not only did members want to see these top ranked players, but they were equally excited to see their friends compete with them.

Gene and his wife, Merrill, stayed with Kathleen and me in our relatively new home in Green Island, just a stone's throw from the courts. This was the first time Gene and I had seen each other since Yale. It would rekindle a friendship which would last until he died prematurely at age sixty-eight. The event was a huge success, and all agreed that it should become an annual event.

I decided that, to select the best players each year, I should visit Forest Hills during the first week of the tournament. Gene took care of tickets and the social activities. This became an annual trip even after we left Columbus. You will recall I referred to this earlier when we were living in Charleston. By simply being around these top players, my game continued to improve.

By the time Kathleen and I arrived in Charleston, I was playing in the Junior Vet tennis tournaments, for the over-35 set. I was ranked as high as number four in this division in South Carolina, with no chance to move up the ladder as the top three players were the tennis coaches at the Citadel, University of South Carolina, and Clemson! However, I thoroughly enjoyed playing with them even if I could never win.

Gene and I stayed in touch as I moved from one resort to another. At every stop, I suggested a Scott tennis event. We produced one at Bay Point, but none at Kiawah as they had Roy Barth as director of tennis, and he had been a tour player of note before taking the position at Kiawah. At PBPCC, we put on several events. Bill Ylvisaker was a friend of Billy Talbert's so Gene and Billy collaborated on some of these. There is a photograph in this book of Gene on one of my polo ponies, hitting a polo ball. He was a terrible rider, but he rarely missed the ball.

Beginning with my stay at PBPCC, I began visiting New York City often and was a member of the Racquet & Tennis Club at 370 Park Avenue. Gene had taken up court tennis after Yale, and showed the same talent at this ancient game as he did at lawn tennis. Soon he would be the US champion. He would have become the world champion, if not for a wily Scot by the name of Howard Angus. Gene could beat all the other court tennis players in the world, but Angus had his number, and Gene never defeated him.

Through Gene, I met George Plimpton, and we visited regularly when I was in New York. They were very interested in a chamber music group, New York Philomusica, and asked me to join them on the board. We held concerts in private homes as well as at Lincoln Center. George and I played court tennis together, and billiards followed by drinks. He died the night before we had a date to play billiards.

George was one of the most interesting, amusing people I have ever met. When I ran my twenty-fifth reunion at Yale, I asked George to come and chair a panel discussion I was organizing entitled, "Quality of Life after Age 50." As always, he had my classmates rolling in the aisles with his questions and stories.

When I was living in Greenwich, I was in New York City often, at the Racquet & Tennis Club, playing pool and court tennis, as well as lawn tennis at the River Club. Gene had sponsored me for the River Club, and I played in the 5:00 p.m. men's doubles matches. I remember one match when Gene was my partner against Owen Williams and another club member. Naturally, I was nervous, as I was clearly the "weak link" in this foursome. As play began, I was hitting the ball as hard as possible. After a few points, Gene stopped play, and asked me, "What do you think you are doing?" I answered that I was simply trying as hard as I could, whereupon Gene asked me, "Do you really think you can bother Owen with your power shots? Take the pace off, and dump the ball at his feet!" Of course, Gene was correct, and we did win the match.

Once, when Dorsey and I were vacationing in Nantucket, Gene and his second wife, Polly, came to stay a few days, with Lucy and Sam, their young children. We had rented a house near the beach in Siaconset. The main activity was tennis at the Casino, which had red clay courts. When we went to the club, the pros recognized Gene, and immediately began badgering me to arrange a doubles game, me and Gene against them. As I remember, these two guys were from California, and were rated in singles and doubles. My youngest son, Billy, was also with us. Time-wise, this was before he had the Bollettieri experience, so his skill level was modest. In fact, I could still beat him. I told Gene about the challenge, and suggested we find him a better partner than me, if he wanted to play them at all. Gene said, "I'll take Billy and play them." This, I thought, would be a disaster, but if Gene was willing, why not?

As the match started, the two pros were bouncing balls off my young son, trying to deny Gene access to the ball. The first set went badly—the pros won 6–2. Meanwhile, I noticed that Gene was coaching Billy after every point. As the second set began, I noticed something different was happening. Gene repositioned Billy, so Gene was getting most of the shots. When Billy did get a shot, he placed it carefully where the opponents could not hit a winner, and Gene could cut off the return, if there was one. Second set to Scott-Elebash, 6–4. Now the pros were visibly nervous. How could this be happening? The third set was a rout, as Gene and Billy won, 6–2.

As Gene came off the court, he said to me, "Well, Bash, that was not my finest playing, but was perhaps my finest coaching success!"

DAVIS CUP IN MOSCOW

In December 1995, the US was playing Russia for the Davis Cup championship in Moscow. Gene and Polly were going, and they invited me and Dorsey to join them. Well, this was a special offer, if you did not mind flying eighteen hours to Moscow in the dead of winter. We quickly accepted, as we both thought this would be the chance of a lifetime. Conventional wisdom said it was relatively safe. So, we accepted, and met Gene and Polly at JFK for the long flight. The first problem was that smoking was allowed on the first leg from JFK to Finland. The smoke in the cabin was beyond belief! The next leg, I was so tired that I was oblivious to the smoke, and when we landed in Moscow, the atmosphere looked like a slimy pool, not air, not fit for human consumption. On the drive into the city center, all we saw was never-ending rows of tract housing, Russian style. There is no way to describe the total desolation, air pollution, and squalor that was the Russian version of suburbia. To our great relief, the hotel (next door to the indoor stadium in which the matches would be played) was at least as good as a second-rate hotel in the US, in some backwater town. If you wanted to lose weight, this was as good as going to the Golden Door back home. In the two weeks we were in Russia, I lost ten pounds, because I could only eat so much cabbage with unknown meat mixed in. The vodka, on the other hand, was fabulous. They drank it in very small glasses, frosted, and the vodka came right out of the freezer. Maybe they had the bottle sitting outside on a window ledge, but it poured like cold Karo syrup. That one lesson has saved me many shaky mornings, because I learned that you could drink vodka straight up, if the glass was very small and you sipped it.

The matches were held in the Olympic stadium, on courts previously used for Scott's Kremlin Cup tournament which had been held a month earlier. The Russian Federation had installed a slow clay surface, perfect for the Russians, bad for the Yanks.

Our team was headed by Pete Sampras, then the best player in the world. Andre Agassi was on the team but not available because of injuries. The Russians had a new kid on the block, Yevgeny Kafelnikov. The other player was a journeyman, Andrei Chesnokov. He had been around a long time, not very well known but potentially dangerous for us Yanks on the slow courts, especially as he was good enough to have reached the semifinals of the French Open on clay.

There were only about a hundred Americans present, and about 18,000 Russians. I remember coming back home, and someone said, "We saw you on the Russian TV. Fred Stolle, broadcasting the match, remarked on air, as the camera panned the American section, 'There is my friend, Peter Elebash, who is a bit frightened to be in Russia under these circumstances!'" There was much drama as Sampras collapsed with cramps after defeating Chesnokov, but was able to recover, win the doubles with Todd Martin, and then crush the Great Russian hope, Kafelnikov, in the deciding match. One night, Jack Hennesey, head of First Boston, invited us and the Scotts to dinner. A restaurant had been recommended to him, outside of the city. He picked us up at the hotel, two cars with drivers. On the trip I tried to make small talk with the driver and his assistant who was in the front passenger seat. I got no response, so I settled down for the twenty-minute drive. There were no street lights, or other lights like you would see in any town in the US. It was dark everywhere except for an ambient light which allowed you to get a vague perception of your surroundings. The cars pulled up in front of some nondescript buildings, with a small fluorescent sign pointing to a restaurant down a flight of stairs.

As we exited the cars, the drivers and their assistants stepped out with machine guns at the ready! Later, I asked our host, Jack, "Are you in some enterprise over here that puts our lives in danger?"

"No," he said, "But they have assassinated thirty bankers over here this year, and I do not want to be number thirty-one." The meal was not worth the journey, but we arrived safely back at the hotel a few hours later.

We then took a flight to St. Petersburg to see the sights. The Hermitage Museum was showing some of the art stolen by the Nazis during WWII, and "rescued" by the Russians. I have had the pleasure of seeing many great works of the French impressionists, but this col-lection had been stored in a dark room, no light, and it virtually glowed when we saw it on display. Dorsey met some Russian artists, and considered their work for US consumption. Their spaces, or flats, were like Fort Knox—walk up five floors, no guard rail, multiple door locks that would confound Houdini, and the art inside was lit by sixty-watt bulbs, with aluminum pie plates for reflectors.

Were it not for Gene, I would most certainly never have visited Russia.

DAVIS CUP IN SPAIN

In the year 2000, after Dorsey and I had parted ways, the US was again playing a Davis Cup final match, this time against Spain. The site was Santander, on the northern coast of Spain, close to the French border. I was alone in Millbrook when Gene called to ask if I would like to join him, with Polly and the kids, on the trip.

My immediate reaction was to decline on the grounds that it was too short notice and—well, I caught myself and said, "Absolutely!" I immediately booked a flight, and called my old buddy, Roy Barth at Kiawah, who was on the Davis Cup committee, to ask if they had any rooms left. Roy was able to accommodate me, and I was off in a very few days. The Spaniards thrashed us on their red clay courts, to the chagrin of our US captain, John McEnroe, but the scenery and company were great. Dining in northern Spain with Pancho Segura, the great ex-Kramer pro, while listening to his endless fund of funny and sometimes outrageous stories, was the experience of a lifetime. Once again, Eugene L. Scott had done something for me that no one else could have done.

I could go on forever with Gene Scott stories. He was a remarkable athlete and court tactician, and a real student of the game. His magazine, *Tennis Week*, was widely read by tennis enthusiasts of all levels. The fact that overflow crowds were left standing on the sidewalk on Fifth Avenue and 92d Street at his memorial service in Manhattan offers evidence of just how much he meant to so many people. Billie Jean King and John McEnroe delivered moving eulogies to a rapt audience. Most of all, he was a true friend, and changed my life in many ways. When he died, I lost interest in keeping up with the tennis world.

HIT THE RESET
BUTTON

The long drive down to Palm Beach from Millbrook gave me time to make a plan. I knew something was missing from my life, I just could not identify what it was. We human beings have come a long way from the days of Galileo, when conventional wisdom was a flat earth being circled by the sun. We understand that the universe is made up of our sun and many planets that circle it in an organized manner. It is an amazing mechanism that operates in a predictable fashion. How did it come into being? If it was the result of a "Big Bang," then what, or who, caused the Big Bang? Furthermore, the human body, the eyes, circulation system, and all the billions of parts involved, did it simply evolve by some random events, or was there an intelligent designer?

I think Darwin's theory of evolution is sometimes misunderstood. All species evolve over long periods of time, or they become extinct. For instance, people breed horses selectively to develop stronger, faster horses. People today are generally taller and stronger than our forefathers of the eighteenth century. Homo sapiens have evolved into a new and improved version of what we were in the past. But I do not believe that some creature emerged from the swamp, and "evolved," developing lungs to breathe air, and then learned to walk on two legs. Random chance does not pull things together, it drives them apart.

I concluded that there must be an intelligent designer, the God of whom we speak. If he could create what we see, then he most assuredly could exert his influence if and when he chooses to do so.

I began to revisit my religious experience in the Episcopal church. I also began to revisit the Bible. Christianity competes worldwide with many other religions, but Christianity has one feature that no other religion has—Jesus. I had heard all about this in Sunday school and in church, but had never really tried to prove to myself that the story was true.

I decided to work on this during my stay in Palm Beach.

My rented apartment was just right for me: one bedroom, living room, small kitchen, and a bathroom. I would be very comfortable here, far better off than I was in the wintry north. I spent time reading, listening to good music, and getting some exercise. I bought a bike, and I had my tennis racquet with me as well. I began playing at the public tennis courts next to the Palm Beach Day school. At first, I hired one of the pros to hit with me. Eventually, I would join some doubles games. In the evening, I went out to one of the many excellent restaurants in town and eat at the bar, while observing the crowd. It was relaxing, and I was glad I had made the trip.

One day I ran into Mike Carney, whom I had met at the River Club in New York. Like me, Mike had worked his way through college playing with a band. We had actually met many years ago, when we both had our bands playing at the Roosevelt Hotel in New York. Some entrepreneur organized an event called "Battle of the Bands," and we were among the many participants. Mike went on to become the leader of one of the most popular society bands in the country. When he isn't on the road with his band, he and his wife, Lisa, live in Palm Beach. Since he didn't have a "day job," he was free to play tennis with me often.

One day, he said, "Peter, wouldn't you like to have company for dinner sometime? Lisa and I have a friend, a widow, and I think you two would enjoy each other." I was reluctant, but asked for details. Her late husband was Blitz Robinson, someone I had known well during my last sojourn in Palm Beach. Blitz lost his money (and consequently his family) during the crash of 1986. In the aftermath, he became a born-again Christian, and established a small ministry serving gangs, addicts, and prisoners in Ft. Lauderdale and later in West Palm Beach. He died from cancer a few years ago. When he told me her name, Jane Dick Robinson, I thought it sounded familiar, but I could not place it at the time. I agreed, and Mike called me later to say she would be expecting my call.

She was very pleasant on the phone, and we made a date for dinner three days hence. The next day, she called me to say something had come up, and if we could change to a later date. I said, "Sure, I guess something better came up, and I don't blame you for breaking our date. After all, you have never met me!" Actually, she had a dinner invitation with friends from London, from her days living there some years ago. We made a joke of it, and I said I would call her the next week. We finally connected, and we went to Amici, a restaurant on the corner of County Road and Royal Palm Way. Shortly after we were seated and ordered drinks, three people entered the restaurant and headed to a nearby table. When Jane saw them, she said, "Please excuse me, I want to say hello to them."

"Certainly," I replied. When she returned to our table, she told me they were her Bible study teachers, Ron and Patsy Fraser, and Nancy de Moss. Then she said, "Did Mikey tell you that I was a Jesus girl?"

"No, but I like the sound of that!"

At dinner, we talked about many things, including her background and her keen interest in her faith. When we got in my car to leave, I remembered that my tape deck was loaded with gospel music. So, I casually turned it on as we were talking. "Is that the radio?" she asked.

"No, it is my tape deck. I love gospel music." She invited me to go to her church on Sunday, and I gladly accepted.

Maranatha is an evangelical church in North Palm Beach. No organ, a live band playing lively music, no vestments, an active congregation clapping hands and raising arms to the sky, totally unlike my old Episcopal church. The pastor, Chris Goins, delivered a powerful gospel message preaching the salvation grace of Jesus

Christ. I had never heard it explained like that, but it definitely resonated with me.

Jane and I continued to see each other, and I was learning more about her road to the faith. I began to study the Bible on my own, and I began attending Ron Fraser's men's Bible study every Wednesday morning.

My empirical analysis of creation convinced me that there was indeed an intelligent designer. No way could it have been a random series of events. If you put eight hundred monkeys in a room with typewriters, they will not eventually create something like the works of Shakespeare. Now, I was examining the life and times of Jesus, as told in the first four books of the New Testament. The Old Testament, I learned, was the history of the Chosen People, their repeated cycle of obedience to their God, followed by disobedience. When I hear someone talk about an angry God, they are talking about his punishment of his people, as they repeatedly reverted to "sin," suffered God's punishment, then repenting. There is a four-hundred-year gap between the Old and the New Testament. The Gospels tell the story of the life and times of Jesus and the New Covenant. All of the New Testament was written during the first century AD. Matthew, Mark, Luke, and John were eyewitnesses to these events. Several thousand more people were also eyewitnesses. There is more written about this story than has been written about any of the Roman emperors. If the Gospel message was not true, why would so many people who had experienced it proclaim it to be true? When Jesus was arrested, the disciples all fled. After the resurrection, they were such ardent believers that most of them died horrible deaths rather than renounce their Christian faith. People do not die in defense of beliefs they do not sincerely believe. That fact, along with the many eye-witnesses, persuades me that Jesus was who He claimed to be, the Son of God sent to save the world. Some say He was just a great teacher, but Jesus, by His own words, does not give us that option. Either he was who He proclaimed himself to be, or He was the greatest fraud ever perpetrated on humanity.

Many Christian believers died at the hands of the Romans rather than renounce Him. By the fourth century, over half of the people living in the known world claimed to be Christians, in spite of severe per-secution. After Emperor Constantine decriminalized Christianity in 324 AD, growth in the faith exploded. Frankly, it was the best deal available. By confessing one's faith in Jesus as your Lord and Savior, you were forgiven, once and for all, for your sins (disobedience). Good works could not buy your salvation, but good works were evidence of your faith. Pagan religions at the time had a series of requirements, an "entry fee" so to speak, if you wanted to be accepted into their belief system. Christianity invited one and all to participate, and guaranteed eternal life to all believers.

Now, many events occurred over the next eighteen centuries that did not reflect well on the church, but today, the Evangelical movement is very strong and growing rapidly. To me, this was extremely appealing.

A BUDDING
RELATIONSHIP

As I heard Jane's life story, I recognized many similarities to mine. She grew up in Chicago, where her father worked for American Airlines. Her aunt Josephine (her mother's sister) lived in Myrtle Beach, South Carolina, where her husband owned a resort hotel on the ocean. Jane's family frequently visited them, and Jane was close friends with Josephine's daughters. Eventually, Jane's parents, Yost and Lillian Cunningham, decided to escape the harsh winters of Chicago, move to Myrtle Beach, and buy a similar hotel on the ocean. Billie, as Jane's mom was known, ran the kitchen operation, and her dad was "Mister Fix It," taking care of maintenance and upkeep in addition to his managerial duties. At an early age, Jane worked behind the reception desk, and was very popular with the clientele and their children. She attended the local high school, and soon was involved in beauty pageants. Scholarship money for college was available to girls who excelled in this, and she eventually was first runner up in the Miss South Carolina competition, part of the Miss America pageant.

She graduated from Queens College in North Carolina, earning a BA degree in English and Education. As graduation day approached, a family friend suggested to her and her family that she should go to New York to start her career in the working world. This was a big move, from South Carolina to the Big Apple, but she accepted the challenge of trying to make it in that highly competitive environment.

She found a position at Wells, Rich, Greene, an advertising agency. She later moved to Foote, Cone & Belding. Over a period of years, she worked for a number of fashion magazines. At one point, she was a fashion editor at *Town & Country*, and was chosen not once but twice to grace the cover. I have those two cover shots framed and prominently displayed in our home today. Her magazine jobs allowed her to travel the world on assignments, and she met many interesting people along the way. It also put some distance between her and her mother, who had a dominating personality, to say the least. When Jane would visit Myrtle Beach, her mom would constantly criticize her hairstyle, her clothes, and general transformation from a South Carolina lifestyle to a New York lifestyle. This would become a constant source of irritation for us with Billie in later years.

Jane and I quickly developed a close relationship. She was a mature Christian, having been led to the faith years before through Bible studies in New York. Remember the three people I met on our first date at Amici? They had come to Palm Beach from New York to start a ministry in one of the most secular environments one could choose. I was a beginner, a baby Christian, but on a steep learning curve. I liked the people I was meeting in this world, and recognized that they had something I desperately wanted—peace of mind. If you know in your heart that you are saved, the thought of the world to come makes the trials and tribulations of this world pale in significance. Mind you, it is not like a lightning strike for most people, but a journey, a learning and questioning process, and continues until we depart these earthly gardens. I had found that for which I had been searching, and I was happy, joyful, over this discovery.

As the time approached for me to head back to Millbrook, I asked Jane to come and check out my life up north. And, we could go through South Carolina on the way so her mother could "inspect" me. I agreed to buy her ticket back to Palm Beach at anytime if she got cold feet. So, in April 2001, we departed on our new venture together.

When I met Billie, I said, "Mrs. Cunningham, please feel free to ask me anything you want, nothing off limits."

She replied, "Call me Billie. How much money do you have, and how much do you make?"

I wasn't prepared for that question to come first, but I stammered something to the effect that I had always managed to live indoors and eat. Like Jane, I had three previous marriages, all of which I presented in executive summary fashion. It was an interesting introduction to the woman who would become my mother-in-law, but the rest of the three-day visit went reasonably well. Billie wanted Jane to stay longer, and join me later. This would be a continuous theme in the years to come. She was always glad to see us (really Jane), but always pitched a fit when we were leaving. She seriously believed that her daughter should spend weeks or months at a time visiting her in Myrtle Beach without me.

HELLO, MILLBROOK!

We had pretty much decided that, barring some major problem, we would marry soon. The idea of living together unmarried went against the grain for us as Christians. I immediately put Jane on display for my Millbrook friends. She was, and remains, tall and beautiful, very much at home in any social situation. Dorsey and I had been divorced for several years, and everybody eventually gets out of the "social jail" which is the penalty for divorcing a popular woman. By then, most of my friends knew that the divorce was Dorsey's choice, not mine. I gave a big cocktail party at the Millbrook Golf & Tennis Club, to formally introduce Jane to Millbrook society. I hired the best of what was left of the Dixieland musicians in New York to play for the occasion. Mike and Lisa Carney, the happy matchmakers, were in NYC and came up to join us. It was a very promising start for us as a couple in Millbrook.

This was the spring of 2001, a year that would be remembered forever because of future events. We settled into my home in Amenia, and met with the minister of St. Peter's Church, Ed Johnson, to discuss our plans for marriage. Episcopals can be sticky about remarriages, but Ed knew me well. I was on the search committee that brought him to Millbrook years ago, and I had been a key voice on the vestry. He quickly recognized Jane's faith, and agreed to marry us in the church. The service was small, only two couples in attendance—Rod and Nancy Lindsay, and Farnham and Anne Collins. We said our vows, and adjourned to a luncheon at the Millbrook G & T Club. I had invited five couples to join our celebration. As we began to socialize with my friends, they noticed the change in me, and became aware of our commitment to our faith. This was foreign to most of them, thereby putting some distance between us as a couple in this secular society. But we were very happy to be together in Millbrook, and looking forward to returning to south Florida for the winter.

We were regular visitors to NYC, staying at the River Club and dining at Swifty's, playing tennis, hanging out at the Racquet & Tennis Club while Jane went shopping, or visiting old friends from her days in New York. The real estate business continued to thrive, and we were living the good life in the country, only a short drive from the bright lights and tinsel of the city.

At some point, it occurred to me that I had not had a physical exam in over three years. I was not aware of any problems, but the responsible thing to do was to get regular checkups. So, late in the summer, I scheduled an appointment. No problems were identified, but my prostate did not feel right to the examining doctor, and he requested I get a biopsy as it could be cancer. My PSA score was only a bit over four, but he still wanted the biopsy.

Jane and I were shocked. I began contacting the best doctors in NYC, and interviewing friends who had undergone various treatments. Surgery was considered the "gold standard" as the surgeon could see what was there and hopefully remove all of the diseased tissue. Radiation was the other option, but not as certain, and surgery was not possible after you had radiation. None of the doctors that I contacted would give me an immediate appointment—call back in two months! As you remember, my daughter, Palmer, is married to a bright young cardiologist, Ethan Weiss, who is a research scientist in San Francisco. He is from Baltimore, where his father was head of the cardiology department at Johns Hopkins, and their best family friend was Dr. Patrick Walsh, the leading authority on prostate cancer. Ethan referred to him as "Uncle Pat." Dr. Walsh's office called me within twenty-four hours to discuss my case. Dr. Walsh, I was told, would be glad to see me in Baltimore, but one of his apostles was now head of that department at New York Hospital. Why not see him since it was so close to home? I told the lady that I had already tried to see him, and was told he was fully booked for the next two months. She said, "Well, call his office in the morning and I think he will see you." The next day, about eleven o'clock, I called Dr. Peter Schlegel's office. The receptionist said, "We were expecting your call, Mr. Elebash. When would you like to come in?"

"As soon as you can schedule me," I replied.

"Can you come in today?" I allowed as how I was in Millbrook, two hours drive away.

"Well, come in tomorrow, as early as you are able." It helps to know people who know people!

Dr. Schlegel saw me within minutes of my arrival in his waiting room. Behind him, on a table, was an autographed photo of Patrick Walsh. He scheduled me for a biopsy for the next day. The biopsy showed a rather advanced case of cancer. We had a long discussion about the relative merits of surgery and radiation. On his recommendation, I opted for the gold standard, surgery. The date was set for early in November. Perfect timing for me, as my sixty-fifth birthday was later in November, and I was eligible to apply for Medicare (and social security) on the first day of my birth month. Prior to surgery, I needed to give blood, in quantity, to be reinjected during the surgery. Also, I needed to take medication and follow a certain diet to be properly prepared. Jane and I prayed for success, but were not frantic as we knew God was in charge. When it was my time, he would take me, not before. So, we went back to our life in Millbrook, awaiting the date for the operation. God does not promise Christians a trouble-free life, but he does promise to give us the strength required to weather the storms.

SEPTEMBER 11, 2001

We were at home in Amenia that morning, and I was working in my home office. My phone rang, and it was Brad Hvolbeck, the broker in Greenwich. "Is your TV on?" he asked.

"No, why?" As I turned it on, the second plane was crashing into the second tower. We will all remember where we were when we received the news. Within a few hours, over three thousand people died in this first ever attack on our homeland.

This was a day that changed the world, especially the USA. Life would never be the same. Everyone was stunned, in a state of disbelief. How could this be happening in the homeland? American attitudes went from shock to sorrow to anger in a matter of days. To quote President Bush, "The people who knocked these buildings down will be hearing from us."

We are all familiar with the aftermath. One good thing that came out of this tragedy was citizens everywhere in the US suddenly developed a keen sense of "situational awareness." In the military, this is one of the first principles of survival. Know what is going on around you and who is in your space at all times. It would take years for things to get back to some sense of normality, and we would pay a heavy price in blood and treasure, going after the roots of terrorism. We have made progress in the battle, but it is far from over.

The first week in November, we went to New York Hospital. I was checked in and we waited for the call to come to the prep area for surgery. Shortly my name was called and within minutes I was in dreamland. When I woke up, Dr. Schlegel was looking down at me on the table, saying he got all the cancer, and that the operation was a success. Later, he told me that the cancer was very close to breaking out and spreading to other parts of my body. I was expected to be released from the hospital in a few days, but another, unrelated problem reared its ugly head—my digestive system shut down. I could not eat, and had to be fed intravenously. It took two weeks to correct this, and I was required to walk, with the pole holding the intravenous fluid rolling alongside me, around the entire hallway system every two hours. One lap took fifteen minutes. Eventually, my digestive system returned to normal, and I was able to go home. In those two weeks, I lost thirty pounds.

Follow-up tests looked good, and I began to regain my strength. It would be months before I felt remotely back to normal. Today, thirteen years later, my PSA is less than one, and I have had no sign of cancer elsewhere in my body. Dr. Schlegel is good, and God is even better!

For the next five years, we were in Florida for the winter months, when Millbrook real estate was dormant and in Newport, Rhode Island, during July and August, when my clientele was typically away on vacation. My real estate business was thriving, but I began to notice a swelling of the ranks of agents. As always is the case, when sales volume increases, the number of agents chasing deals also increases. New agents implored their friends to support them, and those of us who were well established began to feel the pressure. Friendships began to count more than experience and proven track records. Then, the economy faltered, and sales volume decreased to a trickle. Having seen this act before, I began to make plans to withdraw from what had been a very lucrative enterprise. Fortunately, I made a few huge sales on the way out, and happily headed back to Florida.

Jane's mother, Billie, had been in declining heath, and we were regular visitors to Myrtle Beach. She was in her late eighties, bipolar and eccentric, but with her wits about her. We were finally able to persuade her to accept at-home caregivers, but it was a continual battle, as she was hard to please. She was not able to manage her affairs, but resisted turning it over to Jane. This was very stressful for us, as we were always being criticized and verbally abused. Staying in her home was not comfortable, as Billie did not believe in leaving hot water and air conditioning systems on, so we finally announced that, henceforth, we would stay in a nearby motel. Predictably, Billie was furious, and threatened to disown her only daughter. Finally, with the help of Billie's attorney and Jane's cousin, Patricia Ellison, we were able to calm the troubled waters.

Shortly thereafter, it became clear that Billie needed to move into an extended care facility. The caregivers at home could no longer provide all the medical services she required. Jane's aunt, Josephine, had moved to a facility in Wilmington, North Carolina. One of her daughters, Sandy, was married to a heart surgeon there, Hank Marks, and he had a friend who owned a chain of nursing homes. Because her sister was there, she finally agreed to move to Wilmington to be close to her. They were lifelong friends and constant companions in Myrtle Beach. Absent that fact, I am not at all sure we could have pried Billie away from her home.

With Billie happily situated in Wilmington, we breathed a huge sigh of relief. Mom would be receiving excellent care from well-trained nurses. We immediately began a major renovation of her home, not only to clean it up but to make badly needed repairs. Also, there were three rental apartments, owned by the family LLC, in bad need of not only deferred maintenance but professional management. Billie had finally relented, with pressure from Josephine's daughter, Patricia, and Billie's attorney, and she appointed Jane to be the manager of her affairs. What a relief!

Within two weeks of Billie's arrival in Wilmington, Josephine died in her sleep. Billie was heartbroken. The specter of Billie wanting to return to her home in Myrtle Beach reared its head, but all of us simply ruled that out. She accepted the fact that Wilmington was her new home. Her niece, Sandy Marks, and her husband, Hank, were regular visitors, and we greatly increased our visitation, flying up from Florida. For now, the situation was stabilized.

BIG CHANGES

Jane and I gave up our townhouse in Millbrook, and I announced my retirement from the real estate business there. There was no point in staying in Millbrook, with sales of high-priced properties at a standstill and not likely to improve in the foreseeable future. The cost of maintaining a presence in Millbrook no longer made sense for us. Back in 2004, we had sold Jane's condominium in West Palm Beach and upgraded to Trump Plaza where we had twice as much space, full services with valets, concierge, and security. Plus, a view to die for. We enjoy a clear view to the east of Lake Worth (the intercoastal waterway), Palm Beach, and the Atlantic ocean in the distance. We consider this our "terminal home." Many older people stay here rather than going to a nursing home later in life. All one needs to do is hire a nurse to come in and check on you.

As we celebrated the New Year in 2012, we were comfortable that Billie was in the best place for good care, but beginning to be concerned about her finances. Billie was ninety-two years old, and still showing strong vital signs. I began to analyze how to stretch her assets to cover a possible five- to ten-year stay in Wilmington.

One of the assets was a corner lot next door to her home. I informed the neighbors that we would consider a sale, and began to get calls from a local doctor's wife, who was very keen to build a home in that neighborhood. Soon her attorney was calling, but objecting to a price well in excess of fair market value. After much discussion, we finally agreed to a price provided we had a 1031 property exchange clause in the contract. This would give me time to investigate suitable exchange properties, something that could produce a rental income stream. We also had found the best property manager in Myrtle Beach. Fred Goux and his wife, Susan, are complete professionals, managing rentals as well as acting as a broker for sales. Needless to say, living in Florida, we needed on-site expertise, and by the grace of God we found it.

Selling the lot would give us "breathing room" as the proceeds would add about five years to our calculation of Billie's needs. We could not find a suitable exchange property, even though we made offers on several new homes in the area. It needed to be a discounted price to motivate us to make a trade, and the sellers held their ground.

For the time being, money would not be a problem for Billie, so we went on with our lives, planning to visit Billie for Thanksgiving. We were calling her at least five times per week, and she seemed to be reasonably happy in the Brightmore Nursing Home. She was quite popular among the patients and the staff. It was clear to us that she was getting plenty of attention. Hank and Sandy came to see her often, and Patricia with husband Morton Ellison would drive up from Charleston once a month for a visit. Jane was also flying there twice a month.

On November 9, 2012, we spoke to Billie and one of her nurses. All was normal, and Patricia and Morton were coming to visit the next day. The morning of November 10, we were in our kitchen drinking coffee, when one of the nurses called to tell Jane that Billie was having some problems, but no alarm was being sounded. Billie was getting dressed in anticipation of receiving visitors. Shortly thereafter, Morton and Patricia arrived. As we were told, they walked into her room, greeted her, and she closed her eyes and her breathing stopped. She was so calm that Patricia called a nurse in to see what was happening. Billie had passed away.

Patricia called to deliver the news, and we immediately made plans to drive to Wilmington.

Later, we were told by the nursing staff and Hank Marks that Billie was showing negative signs, like very low oxygen levels. She had lived a full, active life, and had passed without any signs of pain or suffering. For this, we were grateful, but it still represented the end of an era for Jane. Within the week, we held a memorial service in Myrtle Beach, and closed down her room in the Brightmore.

LIFE AFTER BILLIE

Back in our home at Trump Plaza, we began the process of settling her estate. Fortunately, her attorney, Eddie Bowers, had taken steps to facilitate this, so it was just a matter of Jane executing Eddie's plan. By the end of January 2013, Jane had dispersed about thirty bequests to those designated in Billie's will, and arranged for Northern Trust in Palm Beach to take delivery of the remaining financial assets which were left to Jane, Billie's only living daughter. Fred Goux took charge of the home and the three apartments, and relieved Jane of all managerial roles.

Jane and I began to rethink our future plans. We no longer needed to make regular visits to Myrtle Beach or Wilmington. We had our lives, so to say, to ourselves for the first time in our eleven-year marriage. We were both heavily involved in our faith-based entities, including Bible studies and First Baptist Church, located only two blocks south of us on South Flagler Drive. Now that we had free time, we began looking for other causes which would interest us. Our calendar year developed as follows: Leave Florida in mid-June for Charleston, South Carolina, to visit Patricia and my son LeGrand's family; after a week's stay, travel on to Newport, taking four days for the drive; stay in Newport until mid-September; drive back to Charleston; and then on to Palm Beach.

Aside from Patricia, we have other friends in Charleston from my days with Kiawah Island. Among them are Pat McKinney and Ben Moore. Ben is a lawyer and is one of my best friends in Charleston. He and his wife, Judy, are terrific folks and we greatly enjoy dining with them. Pat, as you will remember, was an important person in my life during my Kiawah days. When the Kuwaitis sold Kiawah, Pat was invited by the new owners to come back and assume responsibility for real estate sales. Now, some twenty years later, it has been sold again, and Pat is officially retired after a successful and financially rewarding career. He and his wife, Pam, still live in Charleston, and Pat has been an advisor to Governor Haley, serving on the Port Authority board as well as her reelection committee. Now, he is running for lieutenant governor. As always, he and Pam are strong in their faith, and it is such a pleasure for us to visit with them.

Newport is a wonderful place to be during the summer months. Jane and I both have many friends there. We have Bailey's Beach (AKA Spouting Rock Beach Association), the Clambake Club for fine dining, and the New York Yacht Club (Harbour Court) for a fabulous place to entertain. I am also a member of the Newport Reading Room, one of the oldest men's clubs in the country. It is a downsized version of the Racquet & Tennis Club in NYC, without tennis and squash courts. There is a regular group of backgammon enthusiasts on hand every afternoon, from 5:00 to about 7:00 p.m. The wives love the NRR—it keeps the men out of their hair while they rest or get gussied up for dinner, and they know exactly where we are and what we are doing! Too bad Panama City didn't have such a men's club!

LOOKING FORWARD

There is no doubt in my mind that I have experienced a blessed life. It is a wonder I am still alive to write this book. Aside from the normal risks, I participated in dangerous sports, sought a military career that was hazardous, taken many wrong turns along the way that could have ruined my career or left me without any assets. Not for one second do I think this can be attributed to luck. On so many occasions, as one door was being slammed in my face, another door was opening. I have no complaints, and am thankful that the Lord has protected me all this time.

Both Jane and I are reasonably healthy, and we have that peace which comes from knowing that God is, indeed, in charge. We enjoy today, we do not fret over yesterday, and we are not worried about tomorrow. I will celebrate my seventy-eighth birthday this November, and I believe that every day from here on out is a bonus, an opportunity to serve God and his people, namely those in the greatest need. I have become a committed worker/fundraiser for Urban Youth Impact in West Palm Beach. The mission is to change lives in the hood, producing more good citizens and fewer criminals. The statistics for inner-city children, especially African American boys and men, are shocking. Eighty-three percent of the kids live in one-parent homes. The fathers are nowhere to be found. They are much more likely to end up in jail rather than graduating from high school. It is one of the most serious plagues in our country today. Oddly, many philanthropic families prefer to give to schools, hospitals, the arts, and preservation rather than to something like UYI. Either it is not fashionable enough or it appears to be an unsolvable problem, like what's the use, it isn't going to make a difference. Well, it can!

I have seen, firsthand, how lives have been changed so I know it is not a hopeless cause. It just needs more help. To those to whom much is given, much is expected. I am trying my best to get this message out among the people within my reach. Jane and I view this as part of being Ambassadors for Christ wherever we are.

Recently at my Wednesday morning men's Bible study, we heard from a local doctor, a prominent heart surgeon and devout Christian, about the importance, the necessity, of being a disciple for Jesus. Faith without works is weak, and we are called to spread the word. In a venue like Palm Beach, this is not so easy. This is an extremely secular world filled with some of the richest, most successful people on the planet. Unless they have experienced some serious hardship or sickness, they are generally not receptive to Christian witness. However, we understand that our job is to witness, not to convert them. That is God's responsibility.

I have given up on trying to influence our governing classes. The country seems to be drifting toward the European-style socialist model. As Alexis de Tocqueville observed when he visited the US many years ago, "The American republic will endure until the day Congress discovers that it can bribe the public with the public's money." How is it that ordinary people go to Washington as elected or appointed officials, and leave as millionaires? Our recent elections seem to me to be more like American Idol, rather than selecting people with strong credentials, a virtual popularity contest. Only about 50 percent of those eligible to vote actually bother to go to the polls. Not long ago, we saw people in Iraq voting in large numbers, maybe 80 percent of those eligible, even though they risked being killed for doing so. Interviews with people on the street are comical because of the general public's lack of knowledge about our country.

Our universities have eliminated courses on the history of western civilization in favor of politically correct courses. When I was at Yale, we were required to take a range of courses to learn about our history, from the ancient Greeks to current times. This all changed in the late sixties and seventies, as did attitudes in the country. In my opinion, the Vietnam War marked a tipping point, as the general population became disillusioned about the mission and the way the war was being waged. When Lyndon Johnson became president, he, with the advice and consent of Robert McNamara and General Westmoreland, committed us to a full-scale war with a much larger force, yet imposed restrictions on our warriors as to how and where to fight. Johnson once said, as the war was expanding, "Our guys can't bomb an outhouse without my permission." As I mentioned earlier, the lessons of trying to defeat an indigenous enemy 12,000 miles from our homeland are plentiful. It is an exercise in futility. Recently I read Max Boot's book, *Invisible Armies*, about guerilla wars from ancient times up to the present. These lessons were known in the 1970s, but nobody in authority chose to heed them. Lyndon Johnson was a remarkable politician, but a lousy commander-in-chief. Robert McNamara was egotistical, arrogant, and was certain that he had all the answers. General Westmoreland was skilled in tactics that worked in WWII, but not this kind of jungle war.

Recently, we had the opportunity to attend a Luis Palau weekend event at the Breakers Hotel in Palm Beach. I came away encouraged about the future of our country. It was uplifting, positive, and the emphasis was on what we are *for*, not what we are against. In the media, Christians are often portrayed as intolerant bigots, which could not be further from the truth. The Palau team has a worldwide ministry reaching millions of people with the good news of the Gospel, but they also have a local program in their hometown of Portland, Oregon, organizing volunteers to provide, free of charge, all manner of services to schools, public facilities, and local organizations that aid the needy. They have done this in cooperation with the mayor, who is openly gay. While Christians have a biblical view on this subject, this does not stand in the way of working together for the good of the community. While holding traditional Christian values, the Palau team does not let that interfere with Christian outreach. I see that same attitude on display in my home church, First Baptist of West Palm Beach. Our pastor says we want to witness to all people. Jesus came into the world to save sinners, not saints. In fact, there are no human saints, we are all sinners in that we have erred and strayed from God's word. The word sin, of course, means disobedience. No humans are perfect, so we must take that into account when we criticize others.

As I said previously, the Christian walk is a journey, not a destination. I wish I had the skills to communicate this to all my friends, relatives, and those I come into contact with in my daily life. I do try, but only succeed occasionally. However, I will not stop trying. "Hit it with a seven iron, Brother, and keep it in the short grass!"

EPILOGUE

In committing my story to paper, I have intentionally omitted some things which, to me, did not seem important enough to take up several pages. Among those are my experiences shooting grouse in northern England, and skiing in Aspen, Utah, and St. Moritz. As for skiing, everybody has done that. Grouse shooting is not widely known, but is similar to the other upland bird shooting. One episode in St. Mortiz is interesting. You no doubt have seen a recently added Olympic competition, called the skeleton. The origin of this is found in St. Moritz, and is called the Cresta Run. It is one of many sports that the British either invented or established standards for, like polo.

One late night in the bar of the Palace Hotel, I met some foxhunting folks from the UK, and they persuaded me to join them at the Cresta in the morning, for a trial ride. At 2:00 a.m., that sounded like a fine idea. When I arose at 6:00 a.m., I regretted having accepted, but was ashamed to back out. So, I did join them and had three trips down the course. It was terrifying flying down the course head first on a sled that weighted about eighty pounds, with no way of slowing it down. By tilting my head slightly to one side or the other, I could move from one side of the track to the other because of the air flow. The trick is to keep the sled down low on the track, If you began to go high on one turn, you were destined to go even higher on the next one going in the other direction. On my third trip down, I came flying off the course at a turn called "shuttlecock." I later learned that this was a "safety valve" for someone out of control, and therefore on a collision course with a bridge over the course further down the hill. I landed in a snow bank, especially placed just for that purpose. For the history and photographs of this unique creature, Google "Cresta Run St. Moritz." To date, there have been four deaths on the course.

My college friend, Larry Downs, was with me, and his comment was, "Elebash, you are crazy!"

Cousin LeGrand is not mentioned near the end of my story. At the age of seventy-five, he discovered that he had prostate cancer. That, along with a decline in his lifestyle, drove him over the edge. He died of a self-inflicted gunshot to his chest. I have always wondered if I could have prevented this if I had remained in closer contact with him. There was a period of about three months when we did not see each other or speak on the telephone. He was a troubled soul, and never got right with God. It was a tragic way to end it all.

As I was writing about my life experiences, it occurred to me that there is a common condition for man on this planet. We are either heading into a storm, or are in a storm, or are just coming out of a storm. Nobody gets a cushy ride, we all have our share of problems, and the challenge is in how we react to trials. I have learned in my personal journey that, if you have accepted Jesus as your Lord and Savior, He will come alongside you to help you get through the trial. He has a purpose for our lives, and we have a promise of eternal life with him. It is my sincere hope that those reading this book will give God a try. People ask me how I decided to become a Christian. My short answer is, "I tried everything else, and nothing else worked." So, my friends, give God a try. Read John 3:16, my favorite Bible verse, and believe.

The Coin

The Coin

Father's family (He is in the white dress)

Mother's family (she is lower right)

Me and my Whizzer motorbike

My first car—1937 Plymouth

Pensacola Beach, with Johnny Archer and Dad

The BSFH Gang

Coffee High School- # 36

My room at Choate

Student Council—Peter Seed, far left, and
Jeremy Packard, seated right

#26

Trying out drums

Yale Bullpups at Eddie Condon's, NYC

Graduation, and new lieutenant's bars

25th Reunion- George Plimpton seated far right

New Green Beret

Captain Elebash

Pre-jump preparations

Slippery rock, Cashiers, NC

London with Kathleen, c.1966

Running the slalom course

Three generations- L to R:
Me, father and 2 LeGrands

Tennis at Bay Point

Famiy Christmas card

Going after Mr. Fox

"Before the Hunt Begins"

Hugh and Ian, my "tour guides" across country

Kathleen standing near the base of a big jump

The Tipperary Foxhounds

The Master of the Tipperary Foxhounds—Evan
Williams with wife Gill and sons, Hugh and Ian

The Guns, at Clarendon Plantation—Munir
abuHaidar, Farnham Collins, me with our
trusty retriever Deza, and Kyle Spencer

LeGrand Jr. with the day's bag

A BIG turkey—23 pounds

Okeetee Club

Okeetee Club after dinner

Clarendon—an after dinner cigar

Changing dogs

Ruffed Grouse in Maine

Okeetee Club

Clarendon mule wagon

Picnic lunch at Clarendon

Dinner at Clarendon

More Maine Grouse

Shooting Grouse at
Allenheads in Northumberland

The "Beaters", Allenheads

Ready for the drive

My Grouse Syndicate

LeGrand's graduation from St. Pauls

Me with 2 LeGrands at Dorsey's and my wedding reception

Dancing with Palmer at my wedding to Dorsey

Nantucket with Legrand and Allison's
Family and Friends, and Billy

Palmer's graduation from Brown

LeGrand's son with Grandpa, Nantucket

Greenwich Polo—L-R: Me, Michael Levin,
Eresto Trotz and Benjamin Araya

Old Westbury Cup, 1984—Russell
Corey and I battle for the ball

The Pimms Cup, Saratoga, 1983. L-R: Alan
Corey, Benjamin Araya, Julian Hipwood and
me. Gov. Hugh Carey presenting the cup

Old Westbury Cup Champions, 1984—L-R: me,
Hector Barrantes, Paul Rizzo and Ernesto Trotz

Guards Polo at Windsor Park

Sir Raymond Brown, at home in Surrey

Greenwich Polo—L-R: me.E. Trotz,
B. Araya and M. Levin

SCORING CHARGE — Peter Elebash of Boehm Palm Beach charges toward the goal to score in the second chukker of his team's 15-10 win over Glenlivet in the North-Snowden Cup polo match Sunday at the Saratoga Polo Field. —Staff photo by Clark Bell

Saratoga, 1983

Museum Ball, Saratoga—R-L:
Virginia Guest, me and friend

Old Westbury, 1984

Summer in Greenwich, with my 3 children

Tavern on the Green, NYC, with Billy

Crew at Yale

Casa de Campo, c.1983

Greenwich Polo

Billy's motorbike at PBPCC

With Billy in Greenwich 1987

with Maggy Scherer

with Sale Johnson

With Lucy Pearson, daughter of Lord Cowdray

At PBPCC with Billy and LeGrand Jr.

They are growing up

L-R: Maggy Scherer, me and Jorie Butler Kent

Gene Scott at PBPCC

Gene Scott at PBPCC

Gene Scott and Billy Talbert, PBPCC

Gene Scott in Nantucket

The Scott family, Santander, Spain,
2000 Davis Cup Finals

Shooting with Gene Scott,
Tamarack, Milbrook, NY

Allison and LeGrand, fighter pilot school in Jackson, MS.

Legrand's Graduation from Marine OCS at Quantico, Virginia

Graduation from fighter pilot school

The "Sword Arch" at LeGrand and
Allison's wedding, 1995

Rehearsal dinner, 1995

The wedding, Cashiers, NC

Palmer and Ethan's wedding in the
Napa Valley

The "Family Band"

Palmer and Ethan's wedding

Millbrook- L-R: me, Oakleigh Thorne and friend

A Blodgett Dinner Party

Millbrook Dinner Party, L-R: Me, Debbie
Montgomery and Bryant Seaman

Bluegrass music for lunch at Turkey Hollow,
Tamarack Preserve, Millbrook

Deza, Clover and Todi, the guard dogs

Palmer and Billy, Milbrook G &T Club

LeGrand, Palmer and Billy with our dogs

Dutchess Land Conservancy picnic, with
Oakleigh Thorne and Ann Harding

Peter and Beverly Orthwein's Wedding Reception at
the River Club, with the Matchmaker

Deza and I celebrate my 60th birthday

Millbrook Golf & Tennis Club—
Party to welcome Jane to town—
with matchmakers, Lisa and Mike Carney

Sitting in with the band

Christmas Card 2005

Sixth Annual Backgammon Cruise
August 8, 2005

Les Ballard's Annual Cruise

Birthday Cruise for Will—Formerly Billy

Newport Preservation Society Annual Ball

Everglades Club

Newport

David Jeremiah's retreat in San Juan

LeGrand and Allison's children, Chloe
(L) and Hudson, Charleston, SC

Palmer, with her 2 girls

Newport Coaching Weekend

Newport

Bailey, the cat

Nikki Beach, St. Barths